Praise for

"Irene Brand pens a heartwarming romance
with a strong message."
—*RT Book Reviews*

"Ms. Brand writes stories that touch the soul and
bring the reader closer to God with their telling."
—*RT Book Reviews*

Praise for Dana Corbit

"Corbit…writes an alluring tale
of the sharing and the forgiveness
important to our spiritual and corporeal lives."
—*The Oakland Press*

"Ms. Corbit's narrative is infused with emotion,
realism, faith and hope."
—*The Romance Reader's Connection* on *A New Life*

IRENE BRAND

Writing has been a lifelong interest of this author, who says that she started her first novel when she was eleven years old and hasn't finished it yet. However, since 1984 she's published more than thirty contemporary and historical novels and three nonfiction titles. She started writing professionally in 1977 after she completed her master's degree in history at Marshall University. Irene taught in secondary public schools for twenty-three years, but retired in 1989 to devote herself to writing.

Consistent involvement in the activities of her local church has been a source of inspiration for Irene's work. Traveling with her husband, Rod, to all fifty states and to thirty-two foreign countries has also inspired her writing. Irene is grateful to the many readers who have written to say that her inspiring stories and compelling portrayals of characters with strong faith have made a positive impression on their lives. You can write to her at P.O. Box 2770, Southside, WV 25187 or visit her website, www.irenebrand.com.

DANA CORBIT

started telling "people stories" at about the same time she started forming words. So it came as no surprise when the Indiana native chose a career in journalism. As an award-winning newspaper reporter and features editor, she had the opportunity to share wonderful true-life stories with her readers. She left the workforce to be a homemaker, but the stories came home with her as she discovered the joy of writing fiction. The winner of the 2007 Holt Medallion competition for novel writing, Dana feels blessed to share the stories of her heart with readers. Dana lives in southeast Michigan, where she balances the make-believe realm of her characters with her equally exciting real-life world as a wife, carpool coordinator for three athletic daughters and food supplier for two disinterested felines.

A Family for Christmas

Irene Brand
and
Dana Corbit

Love Inspired

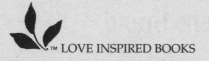 

™ LOVE INSPIRED BOOKS

ISBN-13: 978-0-373-78752-4

Recycling programs
for this product may
not exist in your area.

A FAMILY FOR CHRISTMAS

CONTENTS

Dear Reader,

My friend Dana Corbit and I wish you and your family a Merry Christmas, filled with all of the blessings God made available through the birth of His Son. Dana and I enjoyed working together on *A Family for Christmas.* As you read our novellas, we pray that you will again feel the awe and joy of the coming of the Christ Child.

In my novella, "The Gift of Family," I've brought together two people who love each other, but whose family backgrounds differ so much that it seems impossible for them to find happiness together. Evan Kessler is the product of generations of close family love and Christian witness. Wendy Kenworth is the only child of a broken marriage. Evan offers Wendy the gift of his family, but it's a gift that Wendy believes she will never be worthy to accept. On to Dana....

Through my story, "Child in a Manger," I've tried to show how God uses everyday miracles—this time the arrival of a very special Christmas gift—to bring hope and healing to His children. Allison Hensley has forgotten how to dream, having spent a lifetime caring for others' needs. For Brock Chandler, dreams are a luxury he can't afford. But the arrival of a little "Joy" encourages them to see the possibilities God has for them—including the possibility that they might build a life together.

We hope you enjoy "Child in a Manger" and "The Gift of Family," and that you create wonderful memories with your own family as we celebrate the season of our Savior's birth.

Irene Brand and Dana Corbit

THE GIFT OF FAMILY

Irene Brand

* * *

To the staff of Bossard Memorial Library, Gallipolis,
Ohio, for the efficient research help they've given me.
And to my friends, Torres and Maxine Williamson,
who shared their knowledge of the dairy industry with me.

God sets the lonely in families.
—*Psalms* 68:6

Chapter One

Blue eyes alight with happiness and warmth, Wendy Kenworth eagerly approached the bench where her boyfriend, Evan Kessler, sat. He laid his textbook aside, rising to his feet as his mouth curved into a soft smile of approval. Florida's noontime sun illuminated Wendy's raven-dark hair, sparking a series of iridescent rays. Her head resembled a rainbow appearing suddenly from behind a dark cloud.

An involuntary gasp escaped Evan's lips, and he strode to meet her with a joyful heart. Finally he knew the answer to a question he'd been struggling with since he'd met Wendy three months ago. He loved her, and if the eager, trusting look in her wide azure-blue eyes was any indication, she loved him, too.

Wendy ran into his outstretched arms, and he hugged her tightly. She buried her head against Evan's brawny chest, and he whispered into her fragrant hair, "I love you, Wendy. I want to marry you."

Wendy's heart raced as if she'd just finished a marathon. Her feet seemed to be planted on a cloud. *Evan wanted to marry her!* Having lived in a dysfunctional family most of her life, Wendy couldn't believe that happiness beckoned at last.

Evan held her at arm's length and thought he'd never seen a prettier sight. Wendy's full-lipped mouth curved in a lovely smile. Luminous eyes, enhanced by thick black lashes under delicately arched brows, were the focal point of her oval face. He kissed her dainty nose.

"Will you be my wife?"

"Of course, Evan. This is so sudden." She laughed as she used the timeworn cliché. "You don't mean right away?"

"No, probably not until I've finished the research and written my doctorate thesis. But in the meantime, we can pay a visit to the jewelry store to check out engagement rings. You can visit me in Ohio during our Christmas break, meet my folks and we can announce our engagement to the assembled Kessler clan."

With his arm around Wendy's waist, Evan steered her toward his truck in one of the parking lots of the University of Florida. The surprise was over now, and at his words, Wendy's joy dwindled quickly.

"I don't know if that's a good idea," Wendy said slowly. "Maybe we'd better wait until I tell my mother about us."

As their relationship had blossomed, Evan had been surprised that Wendy was reluctant to let him meet her mother. He'd told *his* family about Wendy as soon as they'd started dating. He'd felt, right from the start, that Wendy was special.

"Let's look at rings, anyway, so I'll know what you like."

Evan opened the door of his pickup truck and boosted Wendy into the passenger seat. He started the engine and turned on the air conditioner, still amazed at the difference in weather between Florida and his native state, Ohio. Imagine using an air conditioner in November!

Before he fastened his seat belt, Evan leaned toward Wendy and pressed a soft kiss on her lips. As she responded shyly, a quick—and disturbing—thought pierced Evan's happiness. He pulled away from Wendy and put the truck in motion.

Evan had suddenly remembered why he'd hesitated to tell Wendy that he loved her. Christianity was the focal point of the Kessler family, but Wendy and her mother never attended church. He wanted a wife who shared his spiritual beliefs. Was he happy or sorry that Wendy's radiant appearance this morning had shocked the words right out of his mouth? With an inward sigh, he realized that he was committed now. Only time would tell if he'd made a mistake.

His abrupt mood swing disturbed Wendy. Evan was always so sure of himself. Now he seemed confused and uncertain.

"What's wrong, Evan?"

"We're going to choose an engagement ring. That's a pretty big step, and naturally, I'm a little shaken."

His teasing, casual tone didn't reassure Wendy. She glanced at Evan's profile, surprised to see a muscle twitching in his right jaw, as if he were upset about something.

"It could be too big a step for us to take without thinking about it," she said reluctantly. "Perhaps you should come home with me this weekend to meet my mother before we make a decision."

"I've already decided. I love you. I want to marry you," he said positively, trying to reassure himself as well as Wendy. "But I *would* like to meet your mother."

He turned into the parking lot of the mall where the jewelry store was located. "We may have problems to overcome," he said, "but all engaged couples face those."

"Especially the Kenworths," she said bitterly. Evan looked at her sharply. Should he have learned more about Wendy's family before giving her his heart?

In the jewelry store, the salesperson seated Wendy and Evan in front of a large display case of diamonds. Wendy's hands grew moist, and she clasped them together.

When the woman went to the vault to bring out additional trays of diamond rings, Wendy whispered, "Evan, we haven't been engaged an hour. Don't you think it's too soon to buy a ring?"

He lifted her hand and kissed her fingers. "We don't have to buy anything today."

The next half hour passed in a daze for Wendy. The saleswoman persuaded her to slip numerous rings on her finger. Her sales pitch about the quality and size of the diamonds confused Wendy. She spoke of various diamond cuts and the shapes of diamonds—round, marquise, oval, pear, princess—on and on, until Wendy's mind whirled and dipped like a carnival ride.

She barely stifled a gasp when she saw the prices of the rings. The only jewelry Wendy owned was the department store variety. She had no idea that an engagement ring could cost thousands of dollars. And the ring she liked best was a "past, present, future" ring with a large diamond in the center and two smaller stones on each side. The ring cost over four thousand dollars, and she wouldn't choose anything that expensive.

Evan watched her closely, probably trying to judge by her expression the rings she favored. When he pressed Wendy to tell him which of the rings she liked, she kept shaking her head. The prices of the rings had overwhelmed her. She and her mother had to struggle to make ends meet on a moderate income. How could Evan, who didn't even have a job, afford any of these rings?

When the clerk excused herself to answer the phone, Wendy whispered, "Evan, I can't make a choice until I know how much you can afford to spend on a ring."

"So far, she hasn't shown us anything I can't afford. My family isn't rich, but we have some money. I keep all the computer data for our farm operation, and I get paid for that. If you find a ring that you like, we'll put it on layaway until we have time to talk to our parents."

Evan was trying to soothe Wendy's fears, but he had a few of his own. What if his parents were troubled over his choice of a bride? He didn't want to do anything to worry them, but he couldn't take back his proposal. Wendy was a sensitive woman, and he wouldn't hurt her by admitting that he'd been hasty in asking her to marry him. Wendy didn't talk much about her family, but he'd learned enough to know that her childhood had been unhappy. One thing he looked forward to, as Wendy's husband, was giving her the opportunity to share the warmth and love of a Christian family.

When Evan's cell phone rang, he said, "I'll go out in the corridor to talk. Go ahead and look over the selection."

He stepped outside the store and touched the talk key on his phone.

"Oh, hi, Mom," he said when he recognized the caller as his mother, Hilda.

Without any preliminaries, Hilda said, "Son, I have bad news. Your father is sick."

"Daddy's sick? You've gotta be kidding. He hasn't even had a cold in years."

He could sense his mother nodding her head in agreement. "That's true, but Karl is sick now. We brought him to Holzer Hospital this morning. He's had a stroke, and the prognosis isn't good."

Fearful images formed in Evan's mind, and he almost dropped the phone. He leaned against a wall to support his trembling knees. "He isn't going to die, is he?" he whispered.

"Lord willing, he won't, but the doctors haven't ruled that out yet," Hilda said grimly.

"I'll come home right away," Evan said.

"Have you finished everything for this semester?"

"Not completely, but I can probably continue the work online." If he had to make a choice between joining his family in a crisis or finishing the work for his

Ph.D., his family would always come first. "I'm coming home."

"We want you to be here. But, Evan..." Hilda hesitated for several seconds. "Your father's left side is paralyzed. Even if he lives, it will be weeks, maybe even months, before he's able to resume working. You'll have some difficult decisions to make."

"Yes, I know. I'll leave right away."

"Drive carefully. Bye."

Evan sank down on the nearest bench, his head in his hands. He couldn't comprehend his mother's message. Karl Kessler was in the prime of life—only fifty-two years old. Evan couldn't envision his brawny, strong father dying or, even worse, being an invalid for the rest of his life.

When Evan didn't return to the jewelry store, Wendy thanked the saleswoman for her help. "We'll make a decision later," she said.

She stepped out of the store and looked around, startled to see Evan's dejected figure on the bench. His chin had lowered to his chest, and his fingers threaded his heavy blond hair.

Rushing to Evan, Wendy sat beside him and took his hand. "What's wrong?"

He lifted his tear-streaked face. The golden freckles across his cheeks and nose stood out in sharp contrast to the pallor of his skin.

"My father's in the hospital. I have to leave for Ohio right away."

"I'm so sorry, Evan. What happened?"

He briefly related the conversation he'd had with his mother. "I can't believe this happened to Daddy. He's always been so strong."

Evan's words aroused old fears and insecurities that Wendy hadn't experienced since she'd met Evan. Panic, strong as a snow blast, froze her heart. Evan had been the best thing that had ever happened to her. When he'd asked her to marry him, she'd felt secure, believing that his love would enfold her forever. Why was she so fearful? Was it because she couldn't understand why Evan would shove his plans for the future on the back burner to rush home because his father was in the hospital?

Panic-stricken, she wondered if Evan ever had to choose between his family and her, would she be in second place? Wendy could hardly bear the pain of it all. For a couple of hours, she'd had a glimpse of paradise. Now in light of Karl Kessler's illness, paradise was only a dim shadow.

Ashamed of putting her own wishes ahead of Evan's sorrow, she said tenderly, "I'm so sorry, Evan. What can I do to help?"

He started to say, "Pray for me," but he doubted that Wendy ever prayed. "You can go with me to my apartment and help pack. I'll take everything with me, since I don't know how long I'll be gone."

Although annoyed because she was thinking about herself when Evan was so upset, his words startled Wendy like the passage of a fire truck in the middle of the night. But Evan needed her compassion now, so she lifted his hand and kissed each finger.

"Sure, I'll help you pack. And don't worry. Your dad will probably be better by the time you get home."

"Did you choose a ring you like?" Evan asked, trying to change the subject.

"Not really. Let's forget about the ring until you come back," she said, refusing to believe he wouldn't return to Florida.

Wendy walked quietly beside Evan to his truck, still wondering why his father's illness had shattered him. Evan was such an even-tempered man; hardly anything ever frustrated him. But in his concern for his father's health, she sensed his total devotion to his family.

Wendy had rarely seen her father since her parents' divorce when she was eight. So it was difficult for her to understand the close ties between Evan and his father. As they drove to the complex where Evan lived, he talked about growing up on the farm, and of the farmwork, the fishing and hunting trips he'd shared with his father. Wendy gained a vague understanding of what she'd missed by not having a father around while growing up.

Everything in Evan's apartment was organized, so in less than two hours, his belongings were gathered into the boxes he'd saved when he'd moved into the apartment in August. As he'd hurriedly packed, Wendy had carried the lighter boxes down the single flight of stairs to his truck.

The empty apartment saddened Wendy because it seemed as if he was leaving for good. Evan's rent was paid through the end of the school year, however, so maybe he would return after Christmas.

Evan's lips were surprisingly gentle when he kissed her goodbye before they left the apartment. Tears trembled on her eyelids, and Evan wiped them away.

"Don't cry, sweetheart, and make it worse for me. I don't want to leave you, but I must be with my family when they need me. I may not be gone long."

He gave her money to pay for a taxi back to her dorm. "If I leave from here, I'll save an hour of driving time. You don't mind taking a taxi, do you?"

She shook her head. "Not at all. You should get started as soon as possible."

Wendy stifled her tears as she stood in front of the apartment building and watched Evan drive away. Once he was out of sight, she leaned against the building and tears of deep frustration trickled down her cheeks. Was this the end of her relationship with Evan?

Chapter Two

A mass exodus of students heading home for the Thanksgiving weekend had almost emptied the dorm where Wendy lived. She welcomed the quietness. Her thoughts still centered around her relationship with Evan, which, in a few months, had catapulted from friendship to a romance.

One of Wendy's closest friends stuck her head in the door to say goodbye before she hurried to catch a bus to the airport. As Wendy gathered the items she'd need over the weekend, she wished she could be as excited as the other students about going home. Her four years at the University of Florida had been the happiest time of her life. Since she lived less than a hundred miles away, she went home at least once a month. If she saw her mother only once or twice during the school year, would she look forward to going home? Holidays at the Kenworth apartment weren't joyous occasions. After her mother had spent long hours working in the department store during the Thanksgiving to Christmas rush, she spent most of her holidays in bed.

Noting that it was almost two o'clock, Wendy shouldered her backpack, picked up a suitcase and hustled to meet a friend who would drop her off at home.

Wendy's friend was a fast driver. They arrived at the apartment building in Jacksonville before Wendy was ready to face her mother. Wendy's excitement over Evan's proposal had been dimmed somewhat by his rapid departure, but she wondered if her mother would sense her daughter's heightened emotions?

Emmalee Kenworth was overly perceptive where her daughter was concerned, and Wendy knew it would be difficult to keep her mother unaware of her inner excitement and turmoil over the day's activities. Evan had made such a difference in her life that Wendy was amazed she'd been able to conceal their relationship from her mother for the past few months. Now that Evan had asked her to marry him, she knew that she must tell her mother about him.

Hand on the doorknob, Wendy stopped and took a deep breath before she entered the combination kitchen-living room of their three-room apartment.

"Hello, dear," Emmalee called. Wendy went into the kitchen area where her mother was placing silverware on the table.

Wendy had inherited her mother's attractive features, but Emmalee Kenworth was only a shadow of the beauty she'd been in her youth. She was excessively thin, and her mouth had a perpetual droop. Emmalee's expertly applied makeup did little to hide the unhappiness in her eyes resulting from her broken marriage. She worked in the women's clothing section at a local department store, and she had her pick of fashionable clothes at a discount, so she and Wendy were always well dressed.

"Dinner will be ready soon," Emmalee said. "I brought sweet-and-sour chicken with rice and salad from the deli. I'll put the meat in the microwave to warm now that you're here."

"That sounds good. I'm hungry."

Wendy brought a pitcher of tea from the refrigerator and poured a glass for each of them before she took her accustomed place at the small table. Emmalee served the food in the deli containers, saying, "We won't have many dishes to wash."

"Are you working tonight?"

"No, thank goodness. Our store has been a madhouse this week. I think people start their Christmas shopping earlier every year. I'm off tomorrow, but, as usual, the day after Thanksgiving will be the busiest day of the year at the store. It's hard to tell when I'll get home Friday night. I have to work Saturday and Sunday, too, so we won't see each other much this weekend."

"That's all right. I have a research paper to finish, and I want to start studying for finals."

Emmalee talked about problems at the store, and Wendy answered when it was necessary. With her mind full of Evan's proposal, and his sudden trip to Ohio, she couldn't think of anything else.

"I've arranged for you to work at the store during the Christmas holidays. I know you'd be bored staying home while I'm away, and we can use the extra money."

Wendy's thoughts strayed, remembering that Evan

wanted her to come to his home during their Christmas break. But considering his father's illness, the invitation would probably be withdrawn.

Realizing that her mother was staring at her, Wendy tried to keep her features composed. She knew she hadn't succeeded when her face colored under Emmalee's suspicious look.

"Wh-what did you say, Mother?" she stammered.

"I asked if you preferred to work in the lingerie or housewares department?"

"I don't know much about housewares, but either place will be okay."

They cleared the table in silence, and Emmalee carried a cup of coffee into the living room. Sitting in her lounge chair, she looked at Wendy, who had curled up on the couch, the television remote in her hand.

"Do you have anything to tell me?" Emmalee asked, an apprehensive look in her eyes. "You've been staring into space most of the evening."

"No. Well, maybe I should tell you," Wendy began uncertainly. Suspecting that her news would hurt and anger her mother, she hesitated, searching for an easy way to explain about Evan. There didn't seem to be an easy way, so she tried a direct approach. "For the past three months, I've been dating a man at the university. He's asked me to marry him."

A groan escaped Emmalee's lips, and her face turned the color of ashes. Alarmed, Wendy bounded off the couch, went to Emmalee and put her arm around her mother's shoulder.

"Mother, are you all right?"

Slowly, Emmalee regained her composure, and shrugged off her embrace. When she looked at Wendy, her eyes were filled with anger.

"How could I be all right when you've sprung such news on me? Are you pregnant?"

The gasp that escaped Wendy's lips sounded loud in the uneasy silence of the room.

"Of course not!"

"Well, what else can I think? You've been dating someone for months and you haven't even mentioned him before this? Suddenly, he asks you to marry him. Who is this man? Why haven't you told me about him?"

Wendy wanted to say, "Because I knew you'd react the way you are now." Instead, she said, "I didn't know how serious he was until today when he asked me to marry him."

"Surely you didn't accept his proposal!"

"Yes, I did."

Emmalee lunged out of her chair as if a bee had stung her and she walked nervously around the room. Stark fear, mingled with anger, clouded her eyes.

"When am I going to meet my future son-in-law?"

"I don't know. He's a graduate student at the university, working toward his doctorate. He plans to teach agricultural studies in a college. His family lives in Ohio. His father is seriously ill, and he had to go home today. He doesn't know when he'll come back to Florida."

Without a word, Emmalee went into her bedroom and slammed the door. Fighting back tears, Wendy turned on the television and stared at the screen the rest of the evening. She had no idea what programs she watched.

* * *

Although, at first, Wendy's news had stunned Emmalee to silence, the rest of the weekend, during their time together, Emmalee grilled Wendy about Evan.

Did he have any money?

If they married, would she move to Ohio?

When did they plan to marry?

And what about me? Are you going to abandon me?

After two days of this, Wendy was in no mood to deal with Evan's problems when he called her mom's apartment. She was more concerned with Evan's feelings for her, rather than his family's troubles, but she did ask immediately, "How is your father?"

"Not good," Evan said grimly. "The doctors have told us he'll live, but his recovery will be slow. He may never regain the strength he had before his stroke. It could take a year for his rehabilitation."

"I'm sorry, Evan."

"I'm sorry, too. Not only for Daddy, but for you and me."

Wendy's joy over his phone call diminished sharply.

"What do you mean?" Wendy asked, a chill starting in the pit of her stomach and pulsing rapidly through the rest of her body. Because of the continual animosity between Wendy and her mother during the weekend, Wendy realized that her love for Evan had taken second place to her reliance on him as a ticket to a way out of her present situation.

"It means I can't come back to Florida next semester to finish my research for the doctoral thesis. I'll have to take over the farm management—there's no one else to do it."

"But you're already registered for next semester!" Wendy said, her body stiff with shock.

"I can probably handle most of the work online. If not, my Ph.D. will have to be postponed."

"What about me?" Wendy's heart seemed to shout as she voiced the question. But she'd lived with her mother's possessiveness long enough to know what it was like to demand attention. Wendy had made up her mind years ago that she wouldn't beg for affection from anyone, and she was irritated that she'd asked the question.

The silence that greeted his comment stabbed at Evan's heart. "We can still be engaged, Wendy. And after you graduate in the spring, we'll be married. You can come here to live."

Live on a farm when she'd fleetingly envisioned being the wife of a college professor! Disappointment turned Wendy into the kind of shrew she despised.

"The Bible says that a man is supposed to leave his mother and father and stick with his wife."

Evan laughed shortly, surprised that she knew anything about the Bible. "When did you learn that?"

"I had to sit through Sunday school and daily Bible readings during the ten years when my grandparents had visiting rights. I still remember some of the things I heard."

"Then you must not have heard that the Bible also says a man is obligated to take care of his family. Wendy, it's my duty to take over the farm until Daddy is better," he said, a pleading note in his voice. "Besides, I want to do it. I love my family."

"More than you love me, apparently."

"But you'll be a part of my family when we're married," he argued, trying to control the pain her words had brought.

"No, thank you, Evan. I'm not keen on being Old MacDonald's wife. Our engagement is off before it ever really started. Maybe it's good I learned your intentions before you bought a ring."

She hung up the phone and fell facedown on the bed, feeling as if the bottom had dropped out of her life. Within one week, she had skyrocketed from boredom to the heights of ecstasy and love, only to be plunged suddenly into the depths of despair. Though she lay on the bed for an hour, with her hand on the phone, hoping Evan would call back, Wendy didn't cry. Her sorrow was too deep for tears.

Evan pocketed his cell phone and walked slowly into the hospital. The thought of marrying Wendy had dominated his mind for weeks. He hadn't considered when they could get married, or even where they would live if they got married. He had planned to combine teaching agricultural subjects at a nearby college or a high school with work on the family farm. When his father retired, Evan would leave teaching and take over the full-time management of the farm.

Of course, Wendy hadn't known that. He had put the cart before the horse. He should have told Wendy about his future plans before he asked her to marry him. His proposal had been too hasty, but if he had waited another year or two, his purpose wouldn't have changed. He loved Wendy, and he wanted to marry her.

Evan was hurt by Wendy's attitude, but he understood why she would be disturbed. Still, he had no choice. The farm had been in the Kessler family for a long time, and it was a tradition that the oldest son always inherited the farmland. Not only was Evan the oldest child in the family, he was the only son.

On the second floor of the hospital, Hilda Kessler sat patiently beside her husband's bed, holding his hand, where she'd been since Evan had arrived home three days ago. Evan stood at the foot of the bed and watched his father's erratic breathing. Karl knew the family when he was awake, but he slept most of the time.

"Mom, please go home and get some rest. Uncle Gavin is coming to spend the night with Daddy."

"I can't leave him."

"He'll be taken to the rehab department soon, on the fifth floor, for a few weeks. You can't spend all of that time at the hospital."

"I know," she agreed, her blue eyes dulled with pain over her husband's illness. "I'm neglecting the girls, but I don't want to leave him."

An hour later, when Gavin Kessler came to sit with his brother, Evan finally persuaded Hilda to leave. Despite her obvious concern for her husband, when Hilda settled into the car beside Evan, and he headed toward home, she said, "What's troubling you, son?"

He hesitated, not knowing how much to tell his mother. She knew he'd been dating Wendy, but he hadn't mentioned their relationship to his mother since he'd returned home. He'd figured she had enough on her mind without becoming embroiled in his problems. But on the other hand, perhaps she needed a distraction from her husband's health troubles.

"A few days ago, I asked Wendy to marry me."

He sensed the oblique glance his mother sent in his direction. "And?"

"She accepted. We were looking at engagement rings when you phoned about Dad."

"If you're engaged, you should be happy about it. Why aren't you?"

Looking at his watch with an ironic laugh, he said, "As of one hour ago, I'm no longer engaged."

Hilda Kessler wasn't one to waste words. She didn't answer, but Evan felt her gaze upon him, waiting for him to continue.

"I called Wendy to tell her I would be staying on the farm until Daddy recovers. She wasn't thrilled about becoming a farmer's wife. She said to forget our engagement."

"Evan, if you want to marry Wendy, don't let Heritage Farm be a burden to you. If I hadn't been a farm girl who'd known the Kesslers all my life, I would have been intimidated by the fact that Karl was wedded to family tradition before he married me. We have good hired help, and we can manage without you until Karl is better. True love is rare. If you're sure Wendy is the one for you, don't let anything stop you."

Evan explained his doubts about Wendy's spirituality, adding, "And from what Wendy says, she hasn't ever had a comfortable family home like we have. If she could only visit us and understand why family tradition and our faith are so important to us, she'd surely understand. I'd invited her to come for Christmas, but with Daddy sick, I don't think it's a good idea."

"I want to meet Wendy, so let's see how your father improves. If he's getting along all right, *I'll* invite Wendy to visit us. And we must pray for Wendy's spiritual awakening."

"I've been praying for her. I've asked her to go to church with me, but she's always made excuses. That's the reason I hadn't proposed to her." With a sheepish expression on his face, he admitted, "But I got carried away a few days ago and asked her to marry me, without considering the consequences."

He remembered vividly how Wendy had looked when she'd walked toward him earlier in the week; he felt as if he were waiting at the altar for her. He realized that much of his love for her stemmed from a physical attraction, but he wanted it to be so much more. He yearned for a marriage like his parents had, united not only physically, but spiritually and emotionally, too.

"Wendy and her mother live alone, and she may not want to leave her mother on a holiday."

"We'll find a way. All things are possible to those who believe. Now that my concern for Karl has lessened, I'll spend more time in prayer for you and Wendy. If it is God's will that you should marry Wendy, He'll provide a way."

Heartened by his mother's support, Evan picked up speed. They left the town of Gallipolis behind them, and headed south on a highway along the Ohio River toward their home.

"I don't know what to do next," he said. "Should I call her, or let the situation rest for a few days?"

"Use your own judgment."

"I want to call right away, but being impulsive has already caused trouble. Maybe I should wait a few days to give her time to decide if our love is strong enough to overcome all barriers."

Although she'd angrily ended the conversation with Evan, Wendy was convinced that he'd get in touch with her. Should she apologize or should he? As the days passed and Evan didn't call, Wendy became more and more distressed. Why had she been so angry with Evan? Was it because she'd been overwhelmed with the possibility of losing him? Yet had she lost him through her own misguided words?

She didn't leave the apartment during the Thanksgiving weekend, fearing that Evan would call and she wouldn't be there to talk to him. Wendy didn't tell Emmalee that she'd broken the engagement. But her mother must have sensed there was trouble because she was more lighthearted than she'd been since Wendy had told her about the engagement.

After her return to the university, Wendy practically lived with the cell phone in her hand, fearing she would miss Evan's call. Throughout the week, she couldn't keep her mind on studying, and she doubted she would pass any of her final exams. In desperation, she decided that if she and Evan were going to make up, she'd have to make the first move. And rightly so, she figured, since *her* bad temper had caused the problem in the first place. She would ask about his father's health, and if he seemed to be angry, she wouldn't prolong the conversation.

After another night of sleeplessness, as soon as she got out of bed, Wendy dialed Evan's cell phone number. No answer. Before she completely lost her nerve, Wendy punched in the number of his parents' home, hoping Evan would answer the phone.

"Kessler residence. Hilda speaking" was the answer she received.

Hilda! Was she speaking to Evan's mother or one of his sisters? For a moment, she couldn't remember their names.

In a timid voice that didn't sound like her own, Wendy asked, "May I speak to Evan?"

"Evan isn't here. He's working in the dairy barn. May I ask who's calling?"

"This is Wendy Kenworth, Evan's friend in Florida. I called to ask about his father."

"Evan has told me about you. Thanks for your concern, Wendy. My husband is doing very well, but he has a long road to recovery. He's in rehab now. We're hoping he'll be home before Christmas."

"I'm happy to hear that. Thanks."

"I'll have Evan return your call."

"I have a ten-o'clock class. I'll be in my dorm room until then."

"Wendy," Hilda said, "Evan told me he'd invited you to visit us here in Ohio. The family would like to meet you. I know your classes will end soon, and you won't go back to school until after the first of the year. Why don't you spend part of your Christmas break with us?"

"I don't think I can. I'm supposed to work during the holidays. I need the extra money to help with my school expenses."

"If you change your mind, let us know. We'd enjoy having you visit. I'll ask Evan to return your call."

He hadn't telephoned by the time Wendy had to go to class, and she trudged across campus. It was agonizing to turn off her phone while she was in class.

She finally received the call at noon, while she was in the cafeteria eating a sandwich.

"Hi, Wendy." Evan's cheerful voice came across the miles. "Sorry I wasn't in when you called before. I'm missing you."

Wendy's heart skipped a beat. He didn't sound angry.

"I'm glad your father is recovering."

"But it's as I told you before—he won't be able to take over the farm interests for several months."

"I should have been more understanding, Evan. I know you're doing what you think is best. Considering the circumstances, maybe it was the best decision to forget our engagement."

With a sinking heart, she heard his answer. "You're probably right, at least for the time being. But I still wish you'd come to visit us during your break. I'll send you a plane ticket if you'll arrange to come."

"My mother—" she started, and Evan interrupted.

"Wendy, you can't seem to understand why I feel it's necessary for me to sacrifice my plans for my family.

Don't you see that you're doing the same thing with your mother? Every decision you've made, since I've known you, has been tempered by how it would affect *her*."

Rather than making her angry, Evan's comment opened Wendy's eyes to the truth. She *was* tied to her mother's apron strings.

Chapter Three

For the rest of the week, Wendy mulled over the invitation to visit the Kesslers. When she went home for the weekend, she'd made up her mind. If she was ever going to get married and have a home of her own, she couldn't be held back by her mother's manipulation. In the years since her divorce, Emmalee could have made a life of her own, instead of depending solely on Wendy's presence to give her life meaning.

Wendy had allowed her mother to dominate her life simply because she wanted to avoid conflict. Would she have the courage to make her own decision now? As she planned how to break the news to her mother, Wendy sensed an extra strength that she hadn't possessed before. What had generated this unusual surge of willpower?

During her annual visits to her paternal grandparents when she was younger, Wendy had gone to church, and she'd heard people pray, but she didn't have a personal knowledge of the power of prayer.

Prayer seemed to be an integral part of Evan's life,

not something he did only on Sunday. He prayed before they ate, even in a restaurant. He prayed for help with his exams. He prayed that God would help him make the right decisions. He didn't start a day without asking for God's direction.

As she waited for Emmalee to come home from work, Wendy wondered if the strange new courage she possessed today was a result of Evan's prayers. Was he praying for her now? It was a comforting thought.

After they'd eaten dinner, and Emmalee had changed into lounging clothes, Wendy pasted a smile on her face, took a deep breath and flexed her fingers in an effort to relax. She couldn't delay any longer.

"Evan and his mother have invited me to visit them during my Christmas break. I intend to go."

"So you've made up with him."

"Yes."

An obstinate expression crossed Emmalee's face. "You aren't going anywhere without me. You have no idea what kind of people they are."

Determined that she wouldn't bend to her mother's will, Wendy said, "I *am* going, Mother. I'm twenty-two. If I'm not old enough to make some decisions now, I never will be."

"Obviously it doesn't bother you that I'll be spending Christmas alone."

Wendy bit her lip nervously, her resolve wavering. *Are you praying, Evan?*

"You have single friends at the store who'd be glad to share Christmas Day with you. You'll be working the rest of the time. I'd like to meet Evan's family. I want to see why he loves his family so much that he'll give up, not only me, but his career to take care of them. And Christmas Eve is very important to the Kesslers. I want to experience that part of the holidays with them."

Emmalee was in no mood to listen to reason. "I've slaved for years to give you a home. Now that you're about to graduate and be on your own, when you could relieve me of some of my financial burdens, you're through with me."

Tears pricked at Wendy's eyelids. She felt like she was ten again, but she clenched her fists. She focused on Evan's strong features, his loving ways and his prayer life as a lodestar to keep her on the right course.

"I *am* going to visit the Kesslers during the holidays."

If she didn't keep repeating those words, she'd weaken. She had to keep that goal in her mind.

"Very well!" Emmalee said at last. "As much as I've tried to change you, you're just like your father. When you have an opportunity to work for two weeks and help with the expenses, you skip out and leave me holding the bag just as he did."

Wendy considered reminding Emmalee that she'd refused to accept alimony from her husband or any financial help from his family. Instead, Wendy repeated, "I'm going to visit the Kesslers during the holidays."

Perhaps sensing Wendy's determination, Emmalee said no more. With some dignity, she went to her bedroom and closed the door, leaving Wendy with heaviness in her chest and tears in her eyes.

She had always tried to avoid conflict. When she'd enjoyed a visit with her paternal grandparents, she hadn't told her mother about the good times she had, because Emmalee resented her in-laws. When Emmalee had protested that she was going out too much at night, Wendy had stopped dating and had spent the nights at home studying. Actually, that had been a blessing in disguise, for she'd made the honor roll all through high school and had won a full scholarship to college.

She'd initiated conflict with Evan, and now that they'd reconciled, she was at odds with her mother. What was wrong with her that she seemed to plant discord no matter what she did? But since she'd won the battle, she knew she must move forward before her mother planned a counterattack. She went into her bedroom and dialed Evan's number.

Happiness was evident in Evan's voice when she told him she intended to come to Ohio for Christmas.

"You'll be finished with classes by the fifteenth, won't you?"

"Yes. My last final is on December twelve."

"Good. That will give me time to arrange for an electronic ticket and send your receipt by express mail. Have you ever flown before?"

"No," she said, "and I'm a little worried about it."

"You can get a plane in Jacksonville, and you'll be flying into the Columbus International Airport. There will be one change, either in Atlanta or Charlotte. I'll choose the easiest route for you."

"Thanks, Evan."

"Since I can't return to Florida for a while, thank *you* for coming to see me. I can't wait to see you."

He wanted to ask how her mother had reacted to the

visit, but Evan thought he might be happier if he didn't know. He settled down to a week of waiting before he could see Wendy again.

Considering his eagerness to be reunited with Wendy, Evan couldn't understand why he took his youngest sister, Olivia, with him when he went to the airport to meet her. Olivia had pestered him for days, wanting to go with him, but he'd resisted her entreaties until the morning he was preparing to leave for the airport.

Overcome with shyness about seeing Wendy, and with the memory of her harsh words still in his mind, he was uncertain of what they'd talk about. Deciding it might be better to introduce Wendy to his family gradually, he told Olivia she could go with him.

His little sister was a special gift to Evan, since she'd been born seventeen years ago on his eighth birthday. The fact that they always celebrated their birthdays together had been a bonding factor. But Olivia's personality made it impossible not to love her because she was as affectionate as a half-grown puppy.

In their baby pictures, Evan and Olivia could have passed for twins; their physical characteristics were similar. Like him, she had blond hair, blue eyes and a sprinkling of freckles on her creamy white skin. Glancing at his sister, who didn't even try to conceal her eagerness to be going to meet her brother's girlfriend, he knew it wouldn't be long before Olivia would be dating, too. Although she was tomboyish and preferred working in the fields rather than in the kitchen, she was tall for her age, quick and graceful and the local boys were already asking Olivia for dates.

Wendy's heart did a little flip-flop, and she stopped in her tracks when she entered the arrivals area and saw that Evan hadn't come alone to meet her. She'd seen pictures of Olivia, so she knew who she was. She'd been looking forward to the three-hour trip from the airport to the Kessler home to determine the status of her current relationship with Evan. That would be impossible with Olivia along.

Wendy cautioned herself to avoid being jealous of Evan's sister. She'd already accepted that, if she married Evan, she would have to share him with his family.

Evan's eyes glowed with welcome, and he hurried toward her. He stooped to drop a soft kiss on her lips. With his arm around her, he led Wendy to Olivia.

Spontaneously, Olivia hugged Wendy. "Oh, you're so pretty. Evan, why didn't you tell us that? I've always wished I had dark hair, but I guess I'm stuck with being a blonde."

"Those freckles would stand out like beacon lights if you had black hair," Evan said, lightly tweaking his sister's nose.

Laughing, Wendy said, "I didn't like my hair when I was a teenager, either. In fact," she said, with a knowing look toward Evan, "I've always been partial to blondes."

"Well, I'm glad to hear that," he said, feigning a leering grimace. He took Wendy's carry-on case. "Let's go and get the rest of your luggage. The weather forecast indicates some snow, and I want to start home. We may have a white Christmas."

"Oh, I hope so," Wendy said, her blue eyes large and luminous. "I've seen snow a few times in our area, but it didn't stick on the ground."

"I can't promise for sure, but I figure you'll see some snow in a few days."

Those words Wendy was destined to remember, since inclement weather had a lot to do with her opinion of Evan's home.

Darkness had fallen when Evan turned off the four-lane highway at the small town of Rio Grande to travel on a curving, narrow road. By that time, Olivia had stretched out on the backseat of the Kessler's sedan and had gone to sleep.

Soon Wendy felt completely isolated in a sea of darkness. They crossed several small streams as they wound through the gently rolling hills. Leafless trees, as well as evergreens, formed a canopy over the roadway. When the headlights illuminated two deer standing in the middle of the road, Evan braked sharply. Wendy's hand flew to her throat. The deer stared into the headlights, and Evan turned off the lights. Wendy cringed in the inky-black darkness, and she moved closer to him, clutching his arm.

"The headlights blinded the deer," Evan explained, tooting the horn a couple of times. He turned the lights on again. The deer jumped a fence and disappeared into the heavy underbrush at the road's edge.

Until they'd left the main highway, Wendy had been

chatting easily, but Evan noticed that she'd become unusually quiet after they'd turned onto the byway. This was probably the first total darkness she'd ever seen. He wondered if this was another hurdle he'd have to overcome if he brought Wendy to Heritage Farm as his wife.

Wendy had envisioned Evan's farm home in a rustic setting, so she was hardly prepared for the magnificence of the floodlit Kessler home standing on a hill overlooking the Ohio River. As they approached along the curved driveway, Evan explained, "My ancestors came here from Germany before the Civil War. Our home was built several years later. The bricks for the house were made right here on our land. They weren't of high quality, so my grandfather plastered the exterior of the house and painted it white."

Green shutters framed the windows of the square, two-story building, and electric candles glowed in each window. Despite her tension, Wendy sensed a welcome. Evan bypassed the front door and went to a one-story ell at the rear of the house.

"Daddy built this wing several years ago for a combination kitchen, family room and three-car garage."

An electric light over the door illuminated the covered entrance where Evan brought the car to a halt before waking Olivia. Wendy braced herself as Evan opened the door for her. Even his comforting hand on her arm didn't calm Wendy's nerves as she went inside to meet his family.

Chapter Four

An involuntary shudder swept through Wendy's body. Had fear or cold caused the reaction? She'd been cold ever since she'd deplaned in Columbus. The strong wind had nearly swept her off her feet and had chilled her thoroughly while they walked to the airport's parking garage.

Evan put his arm around her waist as they stepped inside a spacious room. Wendy drew a deep breath and leaned into his embrace. Two women waited for them. The older woman wore a welcoming smile. The other one stared at Wendy, an aloof expression on her face. A moment of tense silence seemed as long as an hour to Wendy as the women scrutinized her.

Wendy scanned the room. An island divided the kitchen and dining area from the family room. In her brief survey, she saw a large-screen television, two sofas, several chairs and tables, a bookcase and a fireplace framed by a massive mantel displaying many trophies and framed photographs.

"Welcome to our home," the older woman said as she stepped forward and took Wendy's hand.

"Wendy, this is my mother, Hilda," Evan said with unmistakable pride, and Wendy sensed the close bond between mother and son.

Wendy assumed the other woman was Evan's sister, but she didn't offer any sign of welcome. A German shepherd stirred lazily from his place in front of the fireplace and came to greet them. Evan knelt down and rubbed his dense short coat of hair, and the dog nuzzled his face.

"And this is Victor," Evan said. "He's the boss around here."

The dog barked up into Evan's face, and the expression of delight on his face seemed to be a dog grin.

A blast of cold air stung Wendy's legs when Olivia opened the door and carried in a piece of Wendy's luggage. Olivia slammed the door against the strong wind. "Supper smells good, Mom," she said. "I'm starved."

"You're always hungry," her sister said.

"This is my other daughter, Marcy," Hilda said.

"Hello," Marcy said without a degree of warmth in her voice, and turned away toward the kitchen. "I'll finish the salad."

Marcy, too, had blond hair and blue eyes, and Wendy was amazed at how much all three children shared their mother's physical characteristics. Mr. Kessler must also be fair-featured.

With a frown at her oldest daughter, Hilda said, "Olivia, show Wendy to her room, and, Evan, you can bring in the rest of her luggage while I finish supper."

Evan still had his arm around Wendy's waist, and she hated to leave him. He gave her a little squeeze, and she picked up her carry-on bag and followed Olivia into the central part of the house and up the carpeted stairway. The family room had been warm and cozy, but the large hallway was several degrees colder. The carpets, the wall hangings, the draperies and the furniture indicated affluence, and Wendy was uncomfortable. Wendy had never seen such a palatial house. She didn't fit in.

"The guest room is next to mine, and we'll share the bathroom between the rooms. Daddy and Mom sleep downstairs, and Marcy and Evan have rooms on the other side of the hall." As Olivia led the way up the stairway, looking over her shoulder, she whispered, "Don't pay any attention to Marcy. She's always been jealous of Evan's girlfriends."

Wendy stopped in her tracks. She'd been curious about any previous girlfriends Evan might have had, but he had talked so openly about his past and hadn't mentioned any romances, so she'd assumed that he, like herself, had never dated.

"Has he had lots of girlfriends?"

Perhaps realizing she'd spoken out of turn, Olivia said quickly, "I shouldn't have said that. Marcy tells me I talk too much."

Wendy followed Olivia into the square room with ceilings that seemed to be about twelve feet high. She stood in the center of the room, feeling lost in such space.

Watching her closely, Olivia said, "Not to worry. Evan has always had lots of friends, but he's never wanted to marry anyone before. I've heard Mom and Dad fretting about it—wondering if he'd ever have any children. It's tradition for this farm to pass down to the oldest son."

Family traditions that determined an individual's lifestyle before he was even born confused Wendy. Evan's firstborn son was destined to someday own this huge old house whether he wanted it or not. She shook her head in confusion. Her mother had been an only child, and Wendy had no thought of any responsibility toward past or future generations. Wendy knew so little about her father's family that she felt no responsibility to them, either.

"But what if Evan doesn't have a son?"

Olivia shrugged her shoulders. "I don't know! It's never happened."

Wendy was still standing in the middle of the room, feeling bewildered, when Evan entered with the rest of her luggage.

"Mom said that supper will be ready in about fifteen minutes, so you can wait until later to unpack."

Olivia went into her room, and Evan said, "Anything wrong?"

She didn't answer at first, but her face spoke for her. When his blue eyes met hers wistfulness flitted across her features. Her eyes clouded with uneasiness, and her body trembled.

"I don't belong here, Evan," she whispered between uneven gasps. "It was a mistake for me to come."

Gathering her into his arms, Evan held her tightly, and she buried her face on the front of his flannel shirt.

"Of course you belong here. I invited you because I wanted you to meet my family. This farm is my heritage, and I wanted you to love it as much as I do." He tucked gentle fingers under her chin and tilted her head backward. He kissed her on the forehead. "You've had a long day, but you'll feel better once you've had one of Mom's meals. Why don't you take a quick shower and change into a pretty outfit? I'll tell Mom to hold supper until you're ready."

Before he closed the door, Evan favored Wendy with a contemplative glance. She lifted her head and forced a smile to her lips. "I'll hurry, Evan."

Although she was uncomfortable and scared, Wendy didn't want to embarrass Evan in front of his family. She hurried to shower and dress. She chose the warmest pants and shirt she had, knowing that her Florida clothes weren't suitable for this climate. The soft fabric of the velour shirt felt good to her skin and the shade of blue matched her eyes. She brushed her hair and put on long loop black earrings. Taking a last look in the mirror on the antique dresser, Wendy knew that Evan wouldn't be ashamed of her appearance. She hustled down the stairs, determined that, in spite of her inner turmoil and doubts, she would be a pleasant guest so that her behavior wouldn't embarrass him, either.

Chapter Five

As the evening progressed, Wendy learned that she didn't have to pretend to enjoy herself. She really was having a good time. She felt a little disloyal when she compared the deli meals her mother served to the succulent home-cooked roast beef, baked potatoes, green beans and broccoli and cauliflower salad Mrs. Kessler served. The food was mouthwatering, and she was amazed when Evan told her that the beef, potatoes and beans were all products of their farm. The apples for the still-warm pie had grown on a tree in the backyard.

Marcy unbent to talk a little, while all of the Kesslers vied with each other to show Wendy around their home.

"I refer to this as my rogues' gallery," Hilda said with a smile, as she pointed to the wall in the family room featuring pictures of her children from birth to the present. Wendy stared at the picture of Evan with his first birthday cake. When she commented on it, Olivia said, "We get to choose what kind of cake we want and also the menu for our birthday dinner."

"You make the cakes yourself?" Wendy asked Hilda.

"Yes, just like my mother always did for her children."

"But what about your birthday? Who helps you celebrate it?"

"That's one day I don't work at all. Since the children have gotten old enough to take care of themselves, Karl always takes me out for the day. We have dinner, sometimes go to a movie. I get to choose exactly what I want to do. He always buys me a new dress, too, but I pick it out."

Wendy thought of the grocery store cakes her mother bought for her birthday. All she'd ever done for her mother's birthday was buy a card. It seemed strange that birthdays were so special to the Kessler family.

"Look over here," Evan said, taking her hand and guiding her to the opposite wall, covered with plaques and citations. "There are awards the Kesslers have won for their contribution to the farming industry in the state of Ohio." He pointed to a trophy displayed on a small ledge. "This was given to my grandfather for a heifer that won first place in her division at the Ohio State Fair."

"Daddy's livestock have taken some awards, too," Marcy said, pointing to the fireplace mantel where several trophies were on exhibit.

"And how is Mr. Kessler? I'm sorry I waited so long to ask."

"He's improving slowly," Hilda said, "but his doctors have promised us that he'll be home for Christmas."

"I'll take you to see him tomorrow," Evan said. "He's looking forward to meeting you."

For an hour they toured the four large first-floor rooms in the original house and Wendy learned much about the family's history. Victor followed as they pointed out ornately framed portraits of stern-looking Kessler men and their wives. The latest portrait was a colored photograph of Hilda and Karl Kessler, taken on their twenty-fifth wedding anniversary. Momentarily, Wendy wondered if someday her and Evan's portrait would hang on these walls. If she ever became mistress of this house, would she want the faces of long-gone Kesslers staring at her every day?

It was nine o'clock when they returned to the family room, and Hilda said, "I'm sure Evan and Wendy want to be alone since they haven't seen each other for a few weeks. So, let's have our family devotions and give them some time together."

Hilda sat in a rocking chair and took a Bible from the nearby table. "Usually Karl does this," she explained to Wendy, "but I'm privileged to do it while he's away."

Olivia and Marcy sat on the sofa, and Evan and Wendy took chairs close to Hilda. Victor laid his head on Evan's knee.

Hilda put on her glasses. "This week, we're reading verses from the Old Testament prophesying the birth of Jesus. Tonight, I'll read from the ninth chapter of Isaiah.

"'For to us a child is born, to us a Son is given, and the government will be on His shoulders. And He will be called Wonderful Counselor, Mighty God, Everlasting Father, Prince of Peace.'

"Let's think about Jesus as a counselor tonight,"

Hilda continued. "When we have problems that seem too difficult for us to deal with, we can take our concerns to Jesus. He's been a counselor to me during these days of Karl's illness, and my comforter, as well."

Wendy had unwillingly participated in family devotions at her grandparents' home. Her relationship with her father's parents had been tempered by Emmalee's opinion of them. Now she wished she'd listened to what her grandfather had said, so she could more easily fit into Evan's life.

"Do any of you have any requests before we pray?" Hilda said.

"I need help with my final exam tomorrow," Marcy said.

Evan clasped Wendy's hand. "Let's thank Him for Wendy's safe flight and her presence with us."

"There's a new girl at school," Olivia said. "I've tried to be friends, but she's very distant. I'd like to know how to get close to her. I think she's lonesome."

Hilda reached her hands to Evan and Marcy, and Olivia joined hands with her sister and Wendy. Hilda took the requests of her family to the throne of God, and also asked that Karl have a night of rest and that his recovery be rapid. Hilda prayed for God's blessings upon Wendy, and Wendy sensed the conviction that God heard and would answer that prayer.

After she finished praying, Hilda stood and kissed her daughters and Evan. Then she turned toward Wendy.

"May I?" she asked, and Wendy eagerly offered her cheek for Hilda's soft kiss.

Soon Wendy and Evan were alone, except for Victor who lay down on an old quilt in front of the fire and slept. Evan stirred the embers in the fireplace and put on another log. He piled several large cushions near the hearth and motioned for Wendy to join him. As she settled into the soft cushions, Evan sat very close beside her.

Embarrassed now that they were alone for the first time since she'd broken their engagement, Wendy searched for a safe subject. "I've never sat before a fire like this," she said. "It's so cozy, it makes me drowsy."

"I imagine you are tired after that long plane trip, so I won't keep you long, but I wanted to tell you how happy I am to have you in our home. Christmas is always a special time, and it will be even more so with you here."

She didn't want to tell him how out of place she felt, nor was she quite ready to deal with the tenderness and promise she read in his eyes. Wendy didn't doubt that Evan was ready to renew their engagement, but if she took Evan, that meant taking on his family and their heritage. How could she possibly live up to the example of Kessler wives when she'd never experienced the close-knit bonds of a family? Relationships that Evan took for granted were mind-boggling, frightening to Wendy.

The heat from the fireplace felt good on her face and legs, but Wendy's back was chilly. "I didn't realize that Ohio was so cold. I noticed the temperature on an insurance office's clock as we left Columbus, and it was in the twenties. That kind of weather is very rare in Florida. I don't have clothes for this kind of climate."

Evan put his arm around her. "I should have warned

you about the weather. My mind hasn't been working right the past two weeks since Daddy got sick. Some winters our weather is mild, but not this year. The forecast for the next thirty days is for below-normal temperatures. I hope that won't give you a bad opinion of the area. I want you to like it here."

Wendy had spent most of her life apologizing to her mother for some infraction or another, so she didn't know why it was so difficult for her to apologize to Evan, but she knew she had to.

Summoning her courage, she turned to face Evan and lifted her hand to caress his face. "I'm sorry I was so mean to you when you were worried about your father. I wasn't very understanding. Please forgive me, Evan."

"I forgave your words as soon as you said them. I'd been hasty in asking you to marry me when you didn't know what all that would involve. I realize why you were disappointed."

"It wasn't only that. I'd just had a little glimpse of happiness, and suddenly it was gone."

Evan had often wondered about Wendy's family, and he said, "I've noticed this evening that you've seemed frightened and uneasy. We've done our best to make you feel at home, but you're still wary of us. Why?"

"It isn't your family's fault, Evan. It's my problem. I don't know how to accept love and hospitality when it's offered."

"Why don't you tell me about your mother and your home life? Maybe that will help me understand."

So for the next hour, while wind whined around the

old house and flames crackled in the fireplace, content in the circle of Evan's arms, Wendy told him about her childhood. Of the divorce of her parents when she was eight, of her mother's disillusionment with men in general, of her mother's possessiveness that had led to a lonely childhood because her mother didn't encourage her to have friends. Of the two weeks each year when she visited her paternal grandparents, wanting to love them, but refusing to do so because her mother wanted her to hate them as she did.

As she talked, Evan saw beyond her words and caught a glimpse of a lonely child caught in the cross fire between her parents and grandparents. She'd obviously become a pawn in their dissatisfaction with each other.

When Wendy finished, she looked up at him, a piteous expression in her eyes. "You see, Evan, I can never measure up to the kind of person your family expects me to be. I'm obviously not the right person for you—that's why I'm frightened. I had a glimpse of happiness, but I know I'm not capable of achieving it."

He cupped her chin in his palm. "Let's get one thing straight. If you become my wife, you'll be marrying me, not my family. True, I want you to love my family. It will be our life, and I hope we can live it out in Kessler tradition, but if that doesn't work for you, we'll go another way. Until we see how Daddy gets along with therapy, I feel obligated to stay here, but I would never expect you to live anywhere you'd be unhappy. These two weeks will give you time to know us. I won't put any pressure on you for a commitment until you're ready to give it."

Before he released her chin, Evan's lips caressed hers.

"Do you want to tell me why your parents divorced?"

"It was a personality conflict more than anything else. As far as I know, there wasn't any unfaithfulness by either of them. They just didn't get along. He had a quiet, retiring personality, not very affectionate. For some reason, Mother needed constant affirmation that he loved her. She nagged him constantly. To escape, he went to work on oceangoing steamers that kept him away from home for long periods of time. She filed for divorce, giving desertion as the cause. He really didn't desert us—he wanted to pay her alimony, but she refused. She did accept child support, which he paid faithfully."

"Put all of that behind you," Evan said. "I promise you your future will be much better than the past."

Chapter Six

After Evan prepared the fire to hold through the night, he turned out the lights in the family room. Hand in hand they walked upstairs. He paused at the threshold of her room. "I get up at four o'clock to go to the dairy barn, and it will be ten before I come in. Sleep as late as you want and then find your way downstairs."

"Why do you get up so early?" she whispered, not wanting to wake his sisters.

"The cows are milked twice a day. I have to start early, so the afternoon milking can begin by four o'clock."

If Evan didn't finish until ten o'clock in the morning and went back out again at four in the afternoon, she wouldn't see much of him. But she wouldn't make his work any harder by complaining. After all, Evan had put aside his plans for the future to help his father. She realized he was sacrificing, too.

Perhaps sensing her disappointment, Evan said, "We hired a man and his wife to do the second milking, so we can spend every afternoon and evening together. I'd like to take you to see Daddy tomorrow afternoon."

"I'd love that," Wendy said sincerely, wanting very much to see the kind of man Karl Kessler was to cause his son to drop his own plans to take over his work. She lifted her face for his kiss and Evan didn't disappoint her.

Wendy closed the door and a warm glow of welcome surrounded her as she entered the room that had been prepared for her. A Tiffany-style table lamp shed a soft glow over her bed. The bedspread had been removed and the sheets turned down. Wendy laid her hand on the homemade quilt and felt warmth. An investigation revealed that there was a heated mattress pad on the bed. The room was cool, and she dreaded changing into her nightclothes.

An open Bible and a daily devotional book lay on the nightstand. She sat in the rocker beside the bed and picked up the book.

The verse for the day was "Do not be afraid, Mary, for God has been gracious to you."

Wendy read with interest the comment on the Scripture. "Perhaps when the Angel of the Lord appeared to Mary, she may have thought that she was in trouble. She soon discovered that she was being called to a particular mission—to play a part in God's great act of salvation. Was Mary afraid to undertake the mission? Did she feel inadequate to become the mother of the Messiah? Perhaps she sensed that this mission would lead to a difficult life full of heartaches, but she'd said yes."

Wendy rocked slowly, listening to the wind blowing

around the house. Was her situation similar to Mary's? Was it God's plan for her to marry Evan and become the mother of his children? Was God calling her to establish her roots in southern Ohio?

The room was cool, but Wendy unpacked a few of her clothes, slipped into her nightgown and got into bed.

Immediately she felt pampered and loved. The bed was warm, and she sensed the love that the Kessler family had shared in this house for generations. She knew that the same love was hers for the asking.

She turned off the lamp and the room was plunged into total darkness. She sat up in bed frightened. She reached out her hand to turn on the lamp again, but she stopped. What did she have to fear? Evan was only a short distance away.

She resisted the urge to turn on the light and settled deep under the covers. She slipped her hand under the pillow and touched a flashlight. Laughing softly, she turned on the light and flashed it around the room, discovering that the Praying Hands figurine on the nightstand, that she'd thought was an ornament, was really a night-light. She pushed a button on the figurine and a faint light glowed around her. Hilda had thought of everything for her comfort!

The warmth from the heated mattress pad eased her body, and Wendy went to sleep.

Wendy awakened to a soft crackling sound and realized that the room was warmer than it had been when she'd gone to bed. She traced the noise to heating radiators under the windows.

She was so comfortable she didn't want to leave her bed, but she opened her eyes and saw a white piece of paper near the door. She slipped out of the warm bed, retrieved the note and got back under the covers before she read it.

"Good morning, darling," Evan had written. "I hope you had a good night's rest. I'm counting the hours until we can be together again."

Wendy held the note close to her heart. It was six o'clock, and she wondered what time she should get up. She hadn't heard anyone stir, but after a while, she got up, put on a robe and walked to the window. Daylight was breaking softly, and Wendy had her first look at the farmland Evan loved so much.

The house was on a knoll, overlooking wide fields along the banks of a big muddy river. A row of leafless trees marked a large curve in the river, and Wendy had a slight view of wooded hills above the house. Apparently, the farm buildings were behind the house and hidden from her view.

Accustomed to green trees all year round, the landscape looked stark to Wendy. A few oak trees still retained their brown leaves, and there were patches of evergreens in the middle of the forest. Could she ever be content to live in an area like this when she'd grown up in a sunny climate in a state surrounded by sandy beaches, palm trees and lively tourist attractions?

She turned from the window when she heard a slight knock on the adjoining bathroom door.

"Come in," she said, and Olivia opened the door and

peeked in. The girl's eyes were heavy with sleep and her short blond hair was tousled.

"Just checking to see if you're up. We usually eat breakfast at seven, but Mom said to let you sleep late today. I've got to hurry and get ready for school, so I'll take my shower first, if you don't mind."

"Go ahead. Do you ride a bus to school?"

"Yes, and it comes at quarter to eight. This is Marcy's first year in college. She drives to Rio Grande every day. She has a nine-o'clock class so she's ready to leave. I'll hurry so you can get ready for the day."

Wendy went back to bed until Olivia tapped on the door again. "I'm going now, Wendy," she called. "You'll have the upstairs to yourself. See you tonight."

The house seemed unusually quiet after Olivia's running steps disappeared down the stairway. Wendy stayed in bed a few more minutes, alternately dreading and looking forward to the day. She couldn't hear anything except the hissing of the radiators, which wasn't surprising, considering the ten-inch-thick brick walls.

Hilda was in the family room, reading the Bible, when Wendy opened the door.

"Good morning, Wendy," Hilda said. "Did you sleep well?"

"Yes. The bed was so warm and cozy that I hated to leave it. I'm not used to cold weather."

Hilda glanced at Wendy's lightweight slacks, blouse and sandals. "In this area, most of us have three different wardrobes. One set of clothing for winter, another for summer and a third one for spring and fall. Maybe Evan can take you shopping this afternoon."

Wendy shook her head. "I don't want to buy clothes to wear for two weeks in Ohio that I can't use when I go back to Florida. I'll just have to be cold."

"We'll think of something," Hilda said. "What would you like to have for breakfast?"

"A glass of milk and a sweet roll would be fine."

"Well, I can provide that," Hilda said, standing and walking to the kitchen. "Evan drinks coffee and eats a pastry of some kind before he goes to the barn. I have a big breakfast ready for him when he finishes the work. You can eat a little now and then eat with him. How does that sound?"

"Fine. Is there anything I can do to help?"

"Not just yet, but everyone works around here, so I'll soon have something for you to do."

Evan brought the smell of the barn with him when he came into the house, and Wendy wrinkled her nose when she went to the utility room to greet him. She hardly recognized him as the man she loved. He wore stained coveralls and a pair of muddy boots. A wool cap covered his blond curls. When Evan bent to kiss her, his whiskers scratched her face. He seemed like a stranger to her.

In the midst of the pleasure of having Wendy in his home, Evan was aware of the puzzled look on her face, and he guessed the reason for it.

Grinning, he said, "I can't run a farm looking like a fashion model." He hung his cap on a wall rack, removed his boots and shrugged out of the coveralls. In his flannel shirt and jeans, he looked more like the man she knew.

Victor trotted into the room, planted his paws on Evan's chest and barked into his face.

"Hungry, are you?" Evan said. He pushed Victor aside and poured some pet food into a tray and filled the dog's water bowl.

"Is breakfast ready?" Evan asked.

"Yes. Hurry and wash up. Your mother has a lot of good food ready, and I'm hungry."

Wendy had watched with interest as Hilda made biscuits from scratch, prepared low-fat bacon on the grill and scrambled several eggs. When Wendy tasted the biscuits spread with blackberry jelly, she couldn't believe the difference between those biscuits and the ones she'd eaten in restaurants. When she commented on the jelly, Hilda said, "Blackberries grow wild on the farm. I made the jelly last summer."

When they entered the kitchen, Hilda had already had breakfast. She sat at the table and sipped some coffee.

"Wendy and I have been talking about her clothes," she said to Evan.

"I should have told her about the different climate, but I've been so worried about Daddy, I forgot it. I'm sure you don't even own heavy clothes," he said to Wendy.

"That's true. I've never been in a really cold climate before. I knew it would be colder up here, so it's no big problem. I'll only be here two weeks."

"Yes, but there's no reason for you to be cold while you're here," Hilda said. "I don't know why I didn't think of this before. My niece moved to Arizona last year, and she left her winter clothes for my girls. But she's taller than Olivia and Marcy, and although Olivia may grow into them, she can't wear them now. The clothes are clean and hanging in the closet in garment bags. You're about Annie's size, and you're welcome to use the clothes."

"That's a good idea, Mom," Evan said, pushing back from the table to cross his right leg over his knee. "Wendy, if you can wear one of Annie's coats and some boots, your other clothes will be fine."

"They're all right when I'm in the house, but yesterday at the airport, I thought I'd freeze. I'll be glad if I can borrow a heavy coat, and I'll buy a pair of boots. Thanks."

"My niece had some sweatpants and shirts that will be good for lounging around the house, too," Hilda said. "I'll lay out some of Annie's clothes while you're at the hospital."

They found Karl Kessler on the fifth floor of Holzer Hospital, resting after a rigorous morning of physical therapy. The stroke had not only left serious paralysis of his left side, but his speech was impaired, too.

A smile creased his face when Evan and Wendy entered his room. Evan elevated his bed to a reclining position and said, "Daddy, this is my friend Wendy."

Karl extended his right hand and squeezed Wendy's hand with a firm grip. "Happy...to meet... you," he said slowly.

Karl Kessler was a stocky man with powerful shoulders, graying hair and dark blue eyes. Evan didn't look like him now, but Wendy knew this was how Evan would look when he was Karl's age. Although she liked Evan's mother, Wendy was still a bit uneasy around Hilda, but she experienced an instant bond with Karl Kessler. Impulsively, she leaned forward and kissed him on the forehead.

"And I'm happy to meet you, sir. Evan has talked about you a lot."

Tears glistened in Karl's eyes, and he said, "I see... why...Evan...likes you...so much."

As they talked, occasional flashes of pain crossed Karl's face, but he listened eagerly as Evan told him about the farm activities. Evan reported on how many gallons of milk they'd shipped the day before, how they were herding the livestock into barns and sheds because of the cold snap that was predicted.

Karl asked a few questions in his halting voice. And Evan requested his father's advice on several business matters relating to the farm. Wendy didn't have any idea what they were talking about most of the time, but she listened carefully, marveling at the bond of affection and respect between the two men.

During the few times she'd seen her father in her adult years, they'd never had anything to talk about. When he came to see her and took her out to dinner and to buy some new clothes, she didn't know what to say. What would her life have been like if her parents hadn't divorced? Would she have had this warm relationship with her parents that the Kesslers took for granted?

When it was obvious that Karl was getting tired, Evan said, "We'll go now, but Mom is coming back tonight."

He took his father's right hand and clasped Wendy's hands. "Let's have a prayer together," he said. While he prayed, Wendy wondered if the Christian faith the Kesslers shared had made them the affectionate family they were.

The more she was around Evan and his family, the more her love for him increased, but so did her doubts. It may have been a mistake for her to come to Ohio. Considering the differences in their backgrounds, she doubted that she could ever feel at home with his family.

All the time they were with Karl, Evan had an upbeat attitude as he laughed and joked with his father about various farm incidents. But when they returned to the truck, Evan leaned his head on the steering wheel, and his shoulders shook with sobs.

"Oh, Evan!" Wendy said, moving close to him and putting her arms around his heaving shoulders.

"I can't stand to see him that way," he said. "As long as I can remember, he's been a forceful, hardworking man. As a child, I thought there wasn't anything my daddy couldn't do. He's always had a strong voice. He sings in a barbershop quartet, and he's one of the main singers in our church choir. Now he can't even talk."

"But he'll get better," Wendy said. "I was impressed with the little I saw of the hospital's rehab department. Looks to me like he's in good hands."

Evan lifted his head, and Wendy wiped the tears from his face. He leaned toward her and pulled her close. "Thanks for encouraging me, sweetheart. I'm sorry that you won't have the opportunity to see our area in normal times. We're all troubled about Daddy, and according to the local meteorologist, we're in for some record-breaking winter weather. I'd like for you to have seen us as the happy family we usually are. Christmas is one of our most special seasons, and we always have a good time visiting with our far-flung cousins."

Wendy thought it might be better that she was seeing the raw side of life with the Kessler family. If she'd visited during the summertime, when all was well with them, she might not have learned the things she needed to know in deciding her future with Evan.

Chapter Seven

Before they returned to the farm, Evan decided to show Wendy the business section of Gallipolis. "This city was settled by wealthy Frenchmen a few years after the Revolutionary War ended," he explained. "It's always been a prosperous, active city."

He drove along First Avenue to point out Our House Tavern, which had hosted two famous visitors in its heyday—Louis Philippe, Duke of Orleans, who later became king of France, and the Marquis de Lafayette. "The building is a museum now," he said.

"But the Kesslers aren't French?"

"No," Evan said, as he pulled into the parking lot of a pizza restaurant. "I'd mentioned before that we're Germans, but my ancestors were farmers, so they didn't settle in town."

The restaurant wasn't crowded, and the waitress gave them their choice of tables. They chose one close to the window, where Wendy had a glimpse of the Ohio River. They ordered a medium-size pizza and a pitcher of soda.

While they ate, Evan explained more about the history of the area, which was also a part of his heritage.

Before they went home, Wendy stopped at a department store and bought an inexpensive pair of boots that would keep her feet warm during her visit. And she could also use them during rainy seasons at home.

True to her word, Hilda had laid out several of her niece's garments on Wendy's bed. Wendy felt like she was accepting charity, a no-no according to her mother. Emmalee preferred to do without, rather than to take help when it was offered. Wendy had her share of pride, but when she slipped into the calf-length, down-filled coat that had a hood and deep pockets for her hands, any pride she had about accepting hand-me-down clothes disappeared in a hurry. Wrapped in that coat, she felt as if she were sunning herself on a Florida beach.

She put on a sweat suit and went downstairs to meet Evan, carrying the heavy coat over her arm. Evan was waiting to take her on a tour of the farm.

It took them several hours to check out the six hundred acres that made up Heritage Farm. The dairy barn, with four blue silos beside it, where Evan worked each morning, was located close to the house. Attached to the barn was a milking shed for the cattle and a cooling room to preserve the milk. Several sheds, where the cows could find shelter, were built around the dairy complex.

Evan said that most of their cattle were Holsteins, but that in recent years, they had mixed their herd with Jersey cattle. The majority of the animals were still black and white, but the younger stock showed the mixture of Holstein and Jersey blood.

Evan drove first to the river tract where corn and soya beans were raised. Then they traveled slowly through a creek valley passing many outbuildings, employees' homes and pasture fields where cattle and horses grazed.

Before they returned to the house, Evan accessed a narrow road that led up a sharp incline through the woods. They came into a clearing, the site of a brick-veneered small house. Shrubbery bordered a wide porch along the entire front of the house. Snowflakes drifted through the barren tree limbs of the oak trees. A small herd of deer grazed in the clearing. Evan watched closely for Wendy's reaction to the house. He wasn't disappointed.

She stepped out of the truck and looked at the dwelling, her eyes wide with delight. "Evan," she said breathlessly. "You've saved the best for last. This is a storybook setting. Who lives here?"

"Nobody. It was the first home built by my ancestors. It's been vacant since my grandmother died three years ago."

"Let's go inside," Wendy said, starting toward the house.

"It's locked, and I didn't bring the key. We'll look at it another time. We need to get back to the house now. Snow and sleet are forecast for tonight, and I need to help our workers put out extra feed for the cattle."

"Can I help?" she said.

"Maybe, but we'll have to find some work clothes for you."

Back in the utility room, Evan said, "You can keep your sweats on, but take off your coat and your new boots." He rummaged around in a closet until he found a pair of coveralls. "Try these on for size," he said. "I used to wear them before my final growth spurt. We don't throw anything away around here."

He held the coveralls while Wendy stepped into them. "You can roll up the sleeves and legs, and they'll fit better."

He took a blue knitted hat from the closet and put it over her head. She looked so cute in the oversize coveralls that he leaned forward and kissed her lips softly.

He handed a bulky pair of socks to Wendy. "Here are some wool socks, and I'll help you put on these boots."

She sat on a bench to put on the socks and he knelt beside her, so thrilled to have her taking an interest in his work that he could have shouted for joy. He slid the boots on her feet and tied them tightly.

"Stand up and see if you can walk around."

Feeling as if her feet weighed a ton, Wendy took a few experimental steps. Grinning at the difference these clothes made in Wendy's appearance, Evan said, "You look like a farm girl now. Here's some stretchy gloves. They'll fit snug around your fingers."

As they were leaving the house, Marcy drove up. She took one look at Wendy's getup and laughed. "Don't tell me he's roped you into helping with the chores! You'll be sorry."

Wendy quickly defended Evan. "I volunteered to help."

"How'd your exam go?" Evan asked amicably, but he made up his mind to have a private talk with his sister.

"Okay, I guess. That's the last one. I'm free until the first of the year. Have fun," she said, disappearing into the house.

Wendy shivered as the sharp wind pierced the heavy coveralls she wore. This was her first trip into the dairy barn, and Wendy was amazed at the extensive operations. Evan explained that they milked one hundred and fifty cows each day. The milk ran through the automatic milkers to a thousand-gallon cooling tank. Once a day, the milk was pumped directly into a refrigerated truck and hauled to the processing plant.

Wendy and Evan watched as twelve cows entered the milking shed, six on each side of the room. A female employee attached the automatic milkers. The cows ate grain while the milking process continued. When the milkers automatically disconnected from all of the cows, the worker opened two doors. The first cows moved out into the loafing sheds, and another group entered the building to be attached to the milkers.

Wendy found the smells of animal waste, disinfectant and grain overwhelming. She was glad when they went into an office where Evan explained the computer system that kept a history of the herd.

Each cow had a separate page and number in the computer program, as well as a registration number recorded on its ear tag. Records of the milk content and productivity were listed, as well as the reports of samples taken often to prove that the milk was pure. The current history of each cow was available at all times. There was more to dairy farming than she'd ever realized, and Wendy knew that in the future she'd have a greater appreciation for each glass of milk she drank.

They went into the pasture field behind the barn where the cattle and a few horses grazed on the short grass. Evan pointed to some round bales of hay.

"The animals won't be able to reach the grass if it snows, so we'll scatter hay around the corral." He broke the strings on one of the bales and demonstrated how he wanted the work done. "You'll soon get the hang of it."

It wasn't difficult to understand what she should do, but the half-frozen ground sucked at her footwear, and every step she took was an effort. As the boots slipped up and down on her feet, blisters formed on her heels.

Before long Wendy realized that she wasn't cut out to be a farm girl. Her forearms ached from pulling the hay from the bales and scattering it while Evan was busy on the other side of the corral. She was cold, and her feet hurt. She cried in frustration. She wanted so much to be a part of Evan's life and to do the things he wanted her to do, but if this was what marriage to Evan would be like, she couldn't do it.

She'd receive her teaching degree in the spring. As a farmer's wife, could she ever follow her chosen profession? Tears blinded her eyes, and Wendy stumbled over a small rock and fell facedown in the pile of hay she'd just scattered. When Evan reached her, she was sobbing.

"Did you hurt yourself?" he asked, lifting her and cradling her in his arms.

"I…don't…think…so," she said, sniffing between each word.

Evan picked her up and started toward the house.

"Put me down," she protested. "I can walk."

"But I like carrying you," he said.

Hilda met them at the door, with Marcy hovering behind her. "What's happened?" Hilda said.

"Wendy stubbed her toe and fell."

"I knew she wouldn't like it," Marcy said with a smirk.

"That's enough," Hilda said to her daughter in a tone that brooked no argument, and Marcy disappeared into the kitchen.

"I'm all right," Wendy said. "Sorry to make such a fuss. The boots were too big for me, and I couldn't keep my balance."

Evan set her on a bench in the utility room, and he knelt to remove her dirty boots. "She was doing a fine job scattering hay, Mom. The boots were the problem."

Wendy figured that Evan was saying those things to encourage her, but it didn't help.

"The next time you go out to work," Hilda said, "wear my boots—they're closer to your size."

After he'd helped her out of the bulky coveralls, Evan said, "Go upstairs and rest. I'll finish my work and be in for supper soon."

An onslaught of rain against the windows woke Wendy about midnight, followed by wind that whistled and roared as it snaked its way around the house. The strong gusts seemed to shake the building, and when it sounded as if someone was throwing pebbles against the windows, Wendy knew that the dreaded ice storm had reached the valley.

She snuggled down under the heavy blankets and went back to sleep. The next time she awakened, she was cold, and she soon realized why. The electric mattress pad no longer soothed her body with warmth. A chilly black silence enveloped her. She slid her arm under the pillow and pulled out the flashlight. She splayed its beam around the room and pulled the chain on the table lamp, but the light didn't come on. The electricity was off. The continual howling of the wind unnerved Wendy, and she wished she had never left Florida.

Wendy spread an extra blanket on the bed, but she still shivered. She thought more sleep was impossible, but she must have dozed for she roused to a soft knock on the door.

"Yes?" she said.

Evan opened the door and, holding an oil lamp, stepped into the room.

"You're probably aware that we're having an ice storm," he said, "and that we have no electricity. You might as well stay in bed as long as you can. The only heat we'll have is the fireplace and a gas space heater in the family room. We also have a gas cookstove, so we'll be okay."

Wendy sat up in bed and pulled the blankets around her. "How long will the storm last?"

"Hard to tell. We have a battery radio in the kitchen, so we can keep up with what's going on. It's not unusual to lose power throughout the year, so we're prepared for it."

"Aren't your milking machines powered by electricity?"

"Yes, but we have gasoline generators for auxiliary power. I wouldn't want to milk that many cows by hand. When you get up, put on your warmest clothes and your boots and come downstairs."

As he walked to the barn, Evan again bemoaned the fact that Wendy was seeing Ohio at its worst. He should have invited her to come for Easter when flowers bloomed and the trees would be starting to leaf. Instead, she was here, according to the meteorologists, during the hardest winter storm of the century. With this power outage, he'd be spending more of his time in the barn and wouldn't have much time with Wendy. He'd sensed her despairing mood last night, as if she found the farm more than she could tolerate.

When Wendy got out of bed, she soon learned that light wasn't the only amenity she didn't have. She turned on the faucets and didn't get a drop of water. She went into Olivia's room. A mound of blankets on the bed indicated that Olivia, curled up like a kitten, was sleeping in.

"Are you awake?" Wendy whispered.

Olivia uncovered her face. "Uh-huh."

"I can't get any water."

"And you won't get any until the power comes back on. We have a private electric well system."

"What do we do for baths?"

"We'll heat some water on the kitchen stove and take sponge baths. Evan will hook up a generator to the system later on today to run the freezers for a few hours to keep the food from thawing. He might connect to the pump so we can take showers. It just depends on how much he has to do with the cattle."

"During hurricanes we often lose power. But in the part of Jacksonville where I live, we haven't lost electricity for several years."

"There's only one advantage of this storm. Evan told me that school has been dismissed until after Christmas. I'm going to stay in bed. When we don't have electricity, there's not much we can do except sleep."

"I'm going to get dressed and go downstairs. See you later."

Chapter Eight

On her way to the family room, Wendy stopped in the central hall and looked out the window. The countryside was a winter wonderland. Tree trunks, branches and shrubbery were glossy white. Sidewalk and grass were covered with several inches of snow and ice. The power lines were coated with ice. White pine branches littered the ground. Wendy stepped out on the front porch, gasping when she breathed in a suffocating gust of cold air. She heard sounds like gunshots.

She closed the door and hurried into the kitchen. Working by lamplight, Hilda, still dressed in her pajamas and heavy robe, was preparing breakfast.

"I've heated water so you can wash your face and hands," she said. "When the power goes off, we live like pioneers."

"I stepped out on the porch and heard odd, snapping sounds like gunshots."

"The trees are breaking under the weight of the ice," Hilda said. "That's the main reason the power is off— tree limbs are falling on the lines."

Hilda was as bright and cheerful as ever, and Wendy wondered if anything ever phased this woman. Even the family room, which was usually cozy, felt chilly, and Wendy backed up to the fireplace, welcoming its subtle warmth.

"I cooked oats this morning," Hilda said. "I thought we needed a warm cereal. Evan and his dad like oats with cinnamon and brown sugar. That's the way I eat them, too, although my girls pour cold milk over their oats."

"I'll try the cinnamon and brown sugar," Wendy said. "Breakfast food at home is either cold cereal or nothing, but I started eating bigger breakfasts when I went away to college. I'll take care of my breakfast. You're going to be busy enough without waiting on me."

"All right. Coffee is ready, and there's hot water if you want tea. I'm baking a coffee cake, which will be ready by the time you finish your cereal."

In spite of the cold, the room seemed homey while Wendy sat at the table and ate.

"Wonder if this storm is widespread?" she asked. "I probably should phone my mother and let her know that I'm all right. If she hears about this ice storm in Ohio, she'll conjure up all kinds of trouble. I phoned her when I landed in Columbus, but I haven't talked to her since."

"Go right ahead and call anytime you want to—that is, if the lines aren't down," Hilda said. "Tell her we're used to coping with emergencies like these."

When Wendy picked up the receiver, there was no dial tone, but Marcy entered the room and said amicably, "The cell phones should work. I'll get mine for you."

Marcy was fairly friendly when she brought the phone from her room, and Wendy wondered at the change in her attitude. Hilda or Evan, maybe both of them, had probably had a chat with Marcy. Wendy sensed that they hadn't approved of Marcy's coldness to her.

She had no trouble making the call, but there wasn't an answer, and Wendy left a message on the answering machine.

The sleet continued falling until midafternoon when the blustery wind blew the clouds away. The sun spread a mantle of brilliance over the valley that radiated off the ice covering. Wendy squinted when she tried to look outdoors because the dazzling brightness blinded her.

Though the sun was shining, the temperature was still below freezing and the Kesslers prepared for several cold days. The local radio station reported that thousands of southeastern Ohio residents were without power and that it could be a week or more before trees were cleared from all roads and power lines.

"If that's so," Marcy said, "we won't have any power until after Christmas. Does that mean we can't have our family get-together, Mom?"

"Oh, we'll manage somehow," Hilda said. "We'll probably have power in this area before the outlying residents do."

Some of the major highways were blocked by fallen trees or broken electric lines, and the family had to keep in touch with Karl by using cell phones.

Wendy despaired of having any time with Evan, and she wished she had stayed in Florida. He was an hour later than usual coming in for his breakfast, and as soon as he ate, he went back to work.

Wanting something to keep her occupied, Wendy helped Hilda prepare the evening meal. When she couldn't turn on a faucet and get water to wash the salad vegetables, she gained a new appreciation for the benefits she'd always taken for granted. While she worked, she sensed that Hilda was unusually quiet.

Suspecting the reason, Wendy said compassionately, "Are you worried about Mr. Kessler?"

Hilda cast a warm smile toward Wendy. "Not worried exactly, because I know the hospital will take good care of him. He's better off there than he would be at home. They have an auxiliary system that activates within minutes of a power failure. They have emergency plans that go into effect immediately when there's a crisis. There are food and water supplies to last for several days. I phoned this morning, and one of the nurses told me that there will be a full staff at the hospital all the time. The hospital has emergency four-wheel vehicles to bring in their workers. Karl is doing fine, but I miss him very much. He's always stayed close to home, and even if he leaves for a few days, since the girls have been old enough to stay alone, I've gone with him. It's been several years since we've been apart."

Wendy's hands paused over the bowl of lettuce she'd shredded. "Was it very difficult for you to take on all the responsibilities you have here?"

Hilda smiled sympathetically. "Not really. You see,

I just gradually eased into being the mistress of this house. Karl's parents lived here when we were married. We didn't move here until his father got sick, and Karl took over full management of the farm. Besides, I grew up on a nearby farm, and I didn't have to do anything I hadn't done in my parents' home."

Wendy didn't answer, and she applied her attention to the salad again. Hilda turned the meat in the skillet, then she put her arm round Wendy's shoulders.

"Don't worry about it. Love finds a way around even the biggest problems. Evan loves you very much."

Wendy shook her head and swiped at her tears with the back of her hand. "You mustn't have the wrong idea about us. We aren't really engaged, you know."

"He told me that you'd broken the engagement."

"I still feel it was the right thing for me to do. I can never be the kind of wife Evan needs."

"Let Evan be the judge of that."

"For one thing, I don't have the spiritual beliefs that your family has."

"Why not?"

"My grandfather is the minister of a large church in Miami, and Mother has always resented him because he didn't make my father stay married to her. That turned her against Christianity, and my grandparents in particular. She's a very bitter woman, and she's been a huge influence on me."

"Why is she bitter? Have you ever stopped to wonder?"

"Many times! But I'm not very persistent, and she won't talk about her frustrations. It's been easier for me to do what she wanted rather than to cross her. The only time I ever did something she didn't want me to was coming up here for Christmas. And I feel guilty that she'll be spending the holiday alone."

"Let's sit and talk a bit while we wait for Evan to finish work for the night. Christmas really isn't a holiday—it's the commemoration of the birth of Christ. It's been turned into a secular celebration, but not in our family. We do many of the things that others do, like giving gifts, having a big dinner and decorating, but we have some family traditions that we always observe."

"Tell me what they are, so I'll know what to expect."

"Our families were German immigrants to this country, and we still carry out some of their traditions. The Christmas tree is supposedly a German custom started by Martin Luther. Early Christians didn't do much celebrating of Jesus' birth, but one cold and snowy Christmas Eve Martin Luther was walking through an evergreen forest. Stars sparkled down through the snow-covered branches, as if they were a part of the tree itself. He wanted to share this sight with his children, so he cut down a tiny fir tree and carried it home."

"I did a history project on the Hessian involvement in the American Revolution, and I learned that those German soldiers may have introduced the Christmas tree to America."

"That's probably true. Luther and his wife decorated the tree with lighted candles to represent the Christ child as the light of the world. We always have candles on our tree, but the candles are electric ones now."

"Mother and I don't do much decorating at Christmas, but we do have a tree."

"Also we have special German foods, especially lots of bread and cookies from recipes our ancestors brought to this country."

Since most of their Christmas food came from the deli, Wendy didn't comment, but waited for Hilda to continue.

"The highlight of the season for us is the midnight Christmas Eve service, when we celebrate what God did for us by sending His Son into the world to redeem mankind from our sins. Even though I've been a Christian since I was a child, each year when I kneel and take communion with my family, I renew my vow to worship and adore, not only the Christ child, but the crucified Christ. It's a tender moment, and I think after you've worshiped with us, you'll have a new concept of what Christmas means."

"I hope so. After my grandparents got legal rights for me to visit them, I spent two weeks with them each year during the summer. They took me to church, and I do have some knowledge of what your faith is and why it's important to you. But when I turned eighteen, I didn't go back to see them. Rather than hurt my mother, I made a choice and stopped visiting them. The only contact I have with my grandparents is through the check they send me for Christmas each year. I write them a thank-you note, and that's it until the next year."

Hilda stood when she heard Evan enter the utility room. He was accompanied by a slender, gray-haired man.

"Wendy, this is our uncle Gavin, Daddy's brother. His farm adjoins ours."

"Gavin, how did you get here?" Hilda asked. "I thought the roads were closed."

"I came on my ATV," Gavin said as he removed his coat. Hilda took the coat and hung it up. "Evan invited me for supper, but I can't stay long," he said. "I want to get home before dark. I came to see how you were managing." Looking at Wendy, he added with a sparkling laugh. "And I wanted to meet your guest."

Hilda introduced Wendy to Gavin, then she said, "Supper is ready. Wendy, help me put the food on the table. Evan, call your sisters. They're cleaning the living room as best they can without a vacuum cleaner."

"I often come this way for a good meal," Gavin admitted with a smile. "My wife died three years ago, and my two daughters live in Cincinnati, so I get lonely. And hungry!"

"You're always welcome," Hilda assured him.

Wendy liked Gavin Kessler immediately. She saw in him many of the traits she admired in Evan.

After Evan prayed God's blessing on the meal, they gave their attention to the food for a while, then Evan said to Wendy, "Uncle Gavin has spent the past five winters in Florida."

"Oh! In what part of Florida?" Wendy asked.

"I go to several different places, so I can see more of the state. I always wait until after the first of the year to go, but with this kind of weather, I wish I'd gone earlier."

"Uncle Gavin, we couldn't get along without you here for Christmas," Olivia protested.

"Well, don't worry. I'm not planning to leave until this weather improves. I drive down," he explained to Wendy, "so I can have my car. Evan says you live in the Jacksonville area."

"That's right."

"Then I'll make it a point to see you this winter—maybe even take you out to dinner, if Evan doesn't object."

"I'll consider it," Evan said as Marcy and Olivia cleared the table for dessert.

It troubled Wendy that the family took her close relationship with Evan for granted. They knew she and Evan weren't officially engaged. If the rest of her visit continued to prove how inadequate she would be as Evan's wife, they might never be.

Evan was puzzled by his family's attitude, too. He had thought they would oppose his marriage to a nonbeliever, but he remembered what his mother had said when he'd told her about Wendy's lack of faith. "If it is God's will for you to marry Wendy, He'll provide a way." No doubt his mother had spent a lot of time praying for Wendy's salvation, as he had himself.

For the next two days, Wendy didn't see Evan alone, and once she got over being sorry for herself, she realized how difficult it would have been for Hilda and the girls to have weathered this problem without Evan around. She understood now why Evan had to come home.

Chapter Nine

The family room was warm, and the light from the lamps and candles made it the most homelike place Wendy had ever been. Marcy and Olivia found a corn popper and prepared to pop corn over the open fire.

Evan stood on a ladder and searched a cabinet for some board games they'd played as children. He found a Bible trivia game. He shoved it aside because he didn't think Wendy knew much about the Bible, and he didn't want to embarrass her.

"What about playing Chinese checkers?" he said. "We need a game we can all play together."

Wendy had played Chinese checkers with her grandparents, and playing with the Kessler family did make the evening hours pass quickly.

When they finished their fifth game, Evan said, "I can't play anymore. I'm going to the barn and check on things before I go to bed. Want to go with me, Wendy?"

"It's too cold for you to go out," Marcy said to Wendy.

"Not if you put on your heavy coat and boots," Evan

said. "The ground is frozen now and covered with ice. You won't get muddy, but we will have to be careful."

"I'll go," Wendy said.

Evan held her coat and tied on the boots she'd bought. He took a red woolen scarf from a rack and wound it around her head. Her long black hair hung over her shoulders. He'd always thought that the fashionable clothes she wore had added to her beauty, but tonight in this ragtag outfit, she seemed more beautiful than he'd ever seen her.

The ice storm had passed, but the damage it had caused wouldn't be repaired for a long time. "Be careful," Evan cautioned as they stepped outside. He carried a large flashlight in his left hand. "We've cleared a path to the barn, but there still might be slick spots. Hold on to my arm."

When they were about halfway between the house and the barn, Evan turned off the light and put it in his pocket. "I'm sorry we had the storm, but occasionally I do enjoy being in total darkness. We rarely have it completely dark anymore, since we have to keep lights burning for security reasons. When I was a kid, I loved to go outside any season of the year and enjoy the quiet and peacefulness of the night."

Wendy had never known such darkness or quietness. She shrank against Evan, and his left arm pulled her close to him. "I'll turn the light on, if you're afraid."

"No," she said, looking overhead, surprised at the millions of stars blinking down at them. As her eyes adjusted, she realized it wasn't completely dark at all.

A whitish light gleamed around the horizons, and in the east, a distinct glow could be seen.

"The moon is ready to pop over the hills to the east. If you're not too cold, let's watch the moon rise."

He stood behind Wendy and wrapped both arms firmly around her waist. The wind was cold against her face, but she felt a warm glow spread through her, and she gloried in this moment they shared together. She could have stood for hours wrapped, not only in his arms, but in the warmth of his love.

The skyline changed slowly and gently to a tinge of pink dusky rose before the large yellow orb floated into view and started its ascent of the heavens. The stars became obscured in the gorgeous display of the rising moon.

"It's beautiful, Evan. And everything is so quiet. Thanks for asking me to come with you. I've missed being with you today."

He laughed fondly. "Why do you think I asked you? I know there isn't anything very fascinating about a dairy barn, but I couldn't think of any other excuse to have you to myself for a few minutes."

Evan checked the cows that had bedded down in a covered shed area behind the barn, and ran his flashlight around the interior of the barn. "You're very thoughtful of your livestock," Wendy said as they returned to the house.

"They're our responsibility, but also our livelihood. Their milk production will be low because the milking hours will be off schedule, but that's part of farm life. Our income is never as sure as it would be in other vocations."

He wanted Wendy to be aware of the negatives as well as the positives of country living.

The family had all gone to bed when they returned to the house. "I'm going to sleep on the couch," he told her, "because it's supposed to be zero tonight, and I want to keep the fire going."

He walked upstairs with her, lighting her way with the flashlight. The bedroom that had been so warm and welcoming the other nights now seemed cold and un-inviting. Evan splayed the light around the room, and she noticed that someone, probably Hilda, had placed a candle on the bedside table.

"You have a flashlight, don't you?" Evan asked.

"Under my pillow."

"If you're afraid, I'm sure Olivia will gladly share her bed with you."

"No, I'll be all right."

He kissed her, then said, "Mom put extra blankets on your bed, so you'll be warm enough."

The room was cold, and when Wendy took off her shoes and socks and stepped on the floor, she hurriedly put her socks back on and rolled under the covers with-out removing her sweatpants and shirt. She was soon warm enough, but with all of her extra clothing and the added blankets, she could barely move, and turning on her side was a real challenge.

She had hoped that this trip to Ohio would prove that being a farmer's wife wasn't bad at all. The traumatic events of the past few days had convinced Wendy that she didn't have the stamina to be Evan's wife. She doubted that Karl Kessler would ever be strong enough to pursue his normal activities, and if it was up to Evan to become the permanent manager of Heritage Farm, she had no future with him.

She would have to tell him so. She didn't want to hurt Evan, but she couldn't ruin his life by marrying him and then finding out she couldn't be the kind of wife he needed. Besides, she had her own aspirations. Was she willing to give up her dream of teaching to be a housewife and mother?

Her spiritual doubts bothered Wendy, too. In this house she'd experienced hospitality at its best, and she believed the kindness Hilda had shown to her had been motivated by Christian love. She wasn't the kind of bride Hilda would want for her son, yet she'd shown Wendy love as Wendy had never known it before. Wendy supposed her mother loved her, but it had been years since she'd said so, nor had Wendy told her mother she loved her.

In the Kessler house, love wasn't necessarily defined by words—it was an emotion that filled the whole house. Evan deserved that kind of love from his wife. Was she capable of loving her husband and family with a sacrificial love, as Hilda had done? She'd rarely thought about becoming a mother. Her childhood experiences hadn't encouraged her to want children of her own. Yet marriage and children were synonymous in the Kessler family.

* * *

Electric power was restored four days before Christmas. That same day, Hilda received a phone call from the hospital saying that Karl was being discharged. A few hours later he came home in an ambulance, protesting all the way.

The family had rented a hospital bed and placed it in the family room so Karl could be in the center of their activities. Olivia had made a huge Welcome Home, Daddy poster and hung it over the entrance to the house. Marcy drove into town and bought a set of helium balloons and hung them on the head of his hospital bed. Hilda ordered a large bouquet of flowers and placed them on a table beside the bed.

When Karl was wheeled into the house on a gurney and transferred to the bed, he looked at the faces of his happy family and all of the welcome-home gifts. His eyes filled with tears, and he shook his head.

"You should…have put me…in a nursing home until…I can…take care of myself."

"Not as long as I'm able to look after you," Hilda said firmly.

"But…I'm going…to be…a lot of trouble."

"We know that, and I'll hire help to take care of the housework if I need to, but *I'm* taking care of you."

"Why don't you…call off the family…gathering on Christmas night? The family…will understand."

"I've got three young ladies to help me do everything." Hilda bent over him and the look of tenderness in her eyes as she kissed her husband brought tears to Wendy's eyes. "Karl, don't you understand what a loss it would have been to all of us if you'd died? We love you. If you weren't here, none of us would enjoy Christmas. We have even more reason to rejoice this year."

He lifted his good arm and pulled her close. For a moment they stayed cheek to cheek, and a sob rose in Wendy's throat. If she married Evan, would she have this same kind of love?

Now that Karl was home and installed in the family room, there wasn't any place for Evan and Wendy to have any privacy. It was too cold for them to spend much time outside, and the farmwork was keeping Evan busy most of the time. When he kissed her good-night at her bedroom door the second night after his father came home, he said, "I wish I could see more of you. I'm sorry it's working out like this. I thought we could have a lot of time together. Your two weeks will be up before we've had any quality time at all."

"Would I be any help in the barn? I could go to work with you."

Evan didn't know offhand what she could do, but he wasn't going to miss the opportunity.

"That would be great. You could stay as long as you like, and then come to the house."

"Call me when you get up tomorrow morning."

Wendy felt as if she'd just gone to sleep when Evan tapped on her door and woke her the next morning. She forced herself out of bed, washed her face and hands, put on her clothes and staggered down the steps to the kitchen.

Evan had a cup of coffee and a sweet roll waiting

for her. Staring at him with bleary eyes, she was half-annoyed to see him looking as fresh and energetic as he did in the middle of the day.

Yawning widely, she said crankily, "How can you look so perky this early in the morning?"

She hadn't combed her hair, she didn't have on any makeup and she had her sweatshirt on backward. He smothered a smile because he knew if she saw his amusement at her appearance, she'd probably refuse to go with him. And although he didn't expect she would be much help, he wanted her company. These past few days in almost constant companionship with Wendy had reemphasized more and more how much he loved her. He had only one reservation about Wendy becoming his wife—would she ever believe as he did? Should he marry her if she wouldn't raise their children in the Christian faith? Would he break with Kessler tradition and marry her regardless of her religious views?

Evan helped Wendy into so many clothes that she could hardly move. He pulled a hat over her head and handed her a pair of heavy mittens. Although the coffee hadn't done much to rouse her, when Wendy stepped outside and got a jolt of below-zero air, she woke in a hurry.

"How cold is it?" she asked through chattering teeth.

"Five below zero," Evan said as he hustled her along the cleared path to the barn.

Tears formed in Wendy's eyes as she accepted the hopelessness of a future life with Evan. She couldn't live in a climate like this. Tears trickled down her cheeks, making little frozen rivulets on her face. But she didn't want Evan to see so she swiped them away with a mitten before they entered the dairy barn.

Despite their uncertain future, she was ready to help Evan. He asked her to carry a bucket of warm water and follow him as he sanitized the cows' udders before applying the milking machines. But he had a sudden inspiration, and he took her to the calf barn.

There were about fifty calves in little individual stalls, some only a few days old. "Aren't they cute?" she said.

"We have to take the calves away from their mothers soon after they're born, and we feed them by hand." He took a large bottle from a shelf. "Would you like to feed them? I could show you how to mix the milk and other ingredients. You can feed them while I do the milking."

"Feed them like they're babies?"

"Yes. Think you can do it?"

"I'd like to try."

He mixed up a batch of the milk for her, filled one bottle and left her alone. She went to the first stall and eyed the calf warily. The calf wanted his breakfast. He bawled lustily and butted his head against Wendy when she stooped beside his stall as Evan had told her to do. She was pushed off balance, but caught herself before she fell backward. She extended the bottle toward the calf, and he grabbed it in his mouth. In a matter of a few minutes, she refilled another bottle and moved to the next calf. She'd fed ten calves by the time Evan finished his job and came to help her.

Her clothes and shoes were filthy, but Wendy had a

high sense of satisfaction as her feet dragged slowly on the way to the house. Evan had praised her work, and she did believe she'd been a help to him.

Chapter Ten

Perhaps Hilda understood their need to be alone, because after Wendy and Evan showered and ate their breakfast, she asked if they'd do some shopping for her. The days they'd been without power, as well as the extra time it took to care for Karl, had delayed her Christmas preparations.

As they drove into town, Wendy said, "Can I do some Christmas shopping before we go back to the farm? I want to buy some gifts for your family."

"Hasn't Mom explained our gift-giving customs?" he asked with a grin.

She shook her head.

"Our parents taught us when we were kids that there's more to Christmas than receiving. They buy us *one* gift each, and a gift for each other. The cost of the gifts have increased through the years, but it's still one gift each. We children have never given anything to each other that cost money, unless it's something we make and we need to buy the materials to make it."

"That seems very strange to me. My mother always

bought gifts for me—probably more than she could afford."

"Daddy and Mom spend a lot of money, too, but it's always for people who need it more than we do. Each year, they look for two or three projects where their money can be used wisely to take Christmas to others. It's a family project now—all five of us decide whom we should help. As much as possible, these are anonymous gifts."

"Didn't you mind at Christmas when you were a child and your friends received lots of gifts and you got only one?"

"Sometimes. Marcy pouted about it every Christmas for years. But we had all we needed throughout the year, besides a lot of luxuries, most of which we paid for. Our parents paid us for work we did around the farm, and we could buy things ourselves. I paid for my first car, and the ones I've had since then. Marcy bought the car she's driving to college."

"What kind of work did you do?"

"Fieldwork for me in the summer, and I took one year off from college to computerize our records. Daddy isn't into computers, and he paid me well for that year's work," Evan said, his mouth twitching with humor. "I've earned the money I have. The girls helped in the garden. They cleaned the house. Also, we had 4-H projects, showing calves or other animals at the local fair. We accumulated quite a lot of prize money on our animals and showmanship."

"Your life and mine have been so different."

"Dad and Mom put this emphasis on giving rather

than receiving because God gave His Son to redeem mankind from their sins. If it hadn't been for His coming, we wouldn't have Christmas anyway. I hope you won't be disappointed in us, but our emphasis at Christmastime is on celebrating Jesus' birth and the gift of our family."

"But what could you give that doesn't cost any money?"

"You know that big red scarf you've been wearing when we go outside?"

She nodded.

"Marcy made that for me one Christmas. She bought the wool, but she knitted the scarf. Last year, Olivia gave me a card, promising to write to me every week while I was in Florida. Dad has a woodworking shop, and he's made a lot of gifts through the years. I'm not the craftsman he is, but I tinker around with wood sometimes. Last year, I made jewelry boxes for my sisters. It didn't cost any money, because I used scraps of cedar out of Dad's stockpile. I made Dad a pencil holder one year, and a napkin holder for Mom. It's amazing how many things you can give that don't cost any money."

"Since I'm not a Kessler, I can buy some gifts. I especially want to buy some flowers for your parents. They can consider it a thank-you gift for their hospitality if they object to Christmas gifts."

Evan's heart sank a little when she said she wasn't a Kessler. "You do what you like. I just wanted you to know that we're not big on gift buying. We'll do your shopping before we buy what Mom wants from the grocery store."

They went to a store that had a floral shop and, using some of the money her grandparents had sent for her Christmas gift, Wendy ordered an arrangement of red carnations that would be ready in an hour. That gave her time to shop for Marcy and Olivia. She'd noticed they had pierced ears, so she bought both of them a pair of earrings. She wanted to buy a gift for Evan, but she couldn't do that when he was with her.

Hilda and Karl both appreciated the bouquet, which Hilda took to the large dining room and placed in the center of the table. The Kessler family gathering on Christmas night would be hosted in the old house, as it had been done for generations. This idea of doing the same thing over and over every year was mind-boggling to Wendy. But she was a guest, and so for this year at least, she must enter into the festivities.

"What can I do to help?" she asked Hilda.

"You and Evan can go cut the trees this afternoon. We put a big tree in the parlor and decorate it on Christmas Eve. We like to have a smaller one in the family room."

Cut the trees! Preparing the tree in their apartment meant taking the pieces out of a box, assembling them and putting the tree on a table. But life here was different.

Again, Evan bundled her into heavy outerwear for their venture outside.

"Victor always goes to help bring the Christmas trees," Evan said. He whistled, and Victor stirred from his warm place near the fire and galloped into the utility room. He barked at Evan and pawed at the threshold of the outside door.

When Evan opened the door, the dog ran toward the barn. The ice and snow were slowly melting from the onslaught of the bright winter sun, and the pathway was slippery. Evan held Wendy's hand, but his feet hit a slick spot, and he fell backward, pulling her down with him. She landed on his spread-eagled arm. Laughing, he pulled her close, and his lips brushed against hers. They were in plain view of the house, and Wendy hoped no one was looking, but she put her arms around his neck while she enjoyed the sweetness of his kiss. Their eyes locked, and the glint of wonder in his steady gaze caused Wendy's heart to miss a beat.

Victor circled around them, barking excitedly, and when they didn't move, he pounced on them and licked Evan's face.

Laughing, Evan pushed the dog aside. "Spoilsport!" he said to the dog. But he struggled to his feet and helped Wendy to stand.

"I have on so many clothes, I can hardly move," she said.

Evan dusted the snow from Wendy's garments, and shook himself like a dog to get rid of the snow on his back.

"I'm not a very good protector," he said. "Sorry you fell."

One corner of Wendy's mouth pulled into a slight smile, and she looked shyly at Evan. "I'm not complaining," she assured him.

Evan opened the door of a machinery shed near the

barn that contained several tractors and other pieces of farm equipment that Wendy couldn't identify. He backed one of the tractors out of the barn and hooked it to a wagon.

Wendy's attention was drawn to a sleigh that looked as if it would be at home in a Currier and Ives painting. The small sleigh had one seat, and it was painted a shiny black.

"My grandfather bought that sleigh," Evan explained. "If we get enough snow, I intend for you and me to go to the Christmas Eve service in it."

The tractor had a cab, and when Evan opened the door, Victor scrambled inside. Evan helped Wendy into a seat before he settled behind the steering wheel and closed the door.

They passed through three fields before they came to an acreage of cedar trees. Evan parked the tractor, picked up a chainsaw from the wagon bed and motioned Wendy to follow him into the cedar thicket. A rabbit ran out of the evergreens, and with a loud bark, Victor bounded after it.

"We want a tree about seven feet tall," Evan said. "There are twelve-foot ceilings in the living room, and anything shorter than seven feet looks ridiculously tiny. We'll get one about a third that size for the family room."

"I'm surprised you didn't come armed with an ax or a hatchet. It can't be traditional to cut your trees with a chain saw and haul them home on a tractor," she added with a touch of sarcasm.

Evan darted a quick look at her. "Are you getting tired of hearing about our traditions?"

She flushed a little and refused to meet his eyes. "I shouldn't have said that, but I'm drowning in all these things that you do simply because it's been done for the past hundred or so years. You cut your own trees every year, rather than buy fake ones. Maybe newer things are better—like the chain saw. You're wise to use it. It seems to me that it would be stupid to cut a tree with an ax just because your great-grandpa did."

She could tell her words had hurt him, because a nervous twitch appeared in his jaw. He walked on into the forest without answering. How could she tell him that every day brought some new obstacle to show her how unsuitable she was to be his wife? She wished she'd stayed in Florida; then she wouldn't have had these mood swings. She was happy one minute, sad the next. Thinking of Florida made her miss her mother and wonder what she would do on Christmas Day. She'd always considered herself a dutiful daughter, but she shouldn't have left her mother alone on a holiday. And feeling very alone now that she'd made Evan mad, she didn't even have him as a buffer for her guilty feelings.

Evan wasn't mad. He was disappointed and unhappy. It boiled down to one simple fact—he couldn't live without the farm, and Wendy obviously couldn't live with it. He didn't blame her. She had lived in a city all of her life, and she hadn't had a good introduction to rural living. Why did her visit have to coincide with the worst weather southern Ohio had seen in a century? He blamed himself. He should have anticipated this situation and not extended the invitation for a winter visit.

Wendy watched Evan's expression as he searched for the perfect tree. The tree he chose was far from perfect in Wendy's eyes. The tree, which Evan called a Virginia cedar, was a slender, round tree with fine, short branches that drooped so much they couldn't possibly hold heavy ornaments.

Trying to include her, Evan asked her opinion on the trees. But compared to the ones she'd seen in tree lots in Florida, the trees were scraggly and ill shaped. The second tree he chose was a pine, and the branches were sparse. But she supposed the trees would suit the Kesslers.

They returned to the farm in silence. Evan knocked all of the snow from the trees and left them in the machinery shed until time to decorate them. It was Kessler tradition to trim trees on Christmas Eve, so perish the thought that anyone would see an ornament or any tinsel before that.

She knew her attitude was bad, but now that Wendy had started thinking about her mother, she knew she was homesick. Wendy longed for familiar surroundings. If she'd had enough money, she would have bought a plane ticket and gone back to Florida.

Perhaps sensing Wendy's unhappiness, when Hilda and she were alone, Hilda said, "Does your mother have plans for Christmas?"

Wendy bit her lip. "We always stayed at home alone on the holiday. I asked her if she'd invite some of her single friends to spend the day, but I don't think she will."

"Would she come to Ohio if we invite her?" Hilda said, and Wendy looked up quickly.

"I have no idea. I doubt it." Wendy stopped short of saying that her mother couldn't afford to fly to Ohio.

"Perhaps Evan has explained our gift-giving customs?"

Actually, Wendy had heard all she wanted to hear about Kessler customs. She nodded, not trusting herself to speak.

"We consider it Christ-like to give to others at Christmas rather than to spend everything on our own family. I want to invite your mother to come spend Christmas with us at our expense."

"She works in a department store and will be busy working until six on Christmas Eve."

"Well, perhaps she could get a plane early on the morning of the twenty-fifth. She could still be here in time for our family gathering on Christmas night."

"It's nice of you to want to ask her," Wendy said, wondering how Emmalee would react to Kessler traditions and the large family gathering. Her own parents had died before Emmalee had married, and her extended family had never been close. Wendy had a maternal great-aunt, two great-uncles and a few second and third cousins, but she didn't see them often.

"If you'll dial your home phone number, I'll talk to your mother and invite her."

"I'll call from the extension in the utility room," Wendy said.

Emmalee was at home because she'd worked the early shift at the store, and answered on the first ring.

"Hi, Mother. I want to introduce you to Hilda Kessler, Evan's mother. She wants to talk to you."

"Emmalee, we're enjoying Wendy's visit very much, but I feel a little guilty separating you from your daughter at Christmas. Will you come to Ohio and spend the holidays with us?"

Wendy heard Emmalee take a deep breath but not answer. "My husband and I will cover your expenses," Hilda added, "because we'd like to meet you."

Wendy cringed, because she worried Hilda had taken the wrong approach. Wanting to know what Wendy's mother was like before they agreed to her daughter's marriage into the family would seem like a put-down to Emmalee.

Surprisingly, Emmalee said, with a touch of pride in her voice, "I'm not sure I can arrange a visit on such short notice, but it won't be necessary for you to pay my expenses. My department was cited for top sales this year, and I received a sizable Christmas bonus from the store."

"Mother, it would be nice if you'd come," Wendy said. "I don't want us to be apart at Christmas."

She expected Emmalee to tell her that she'd chosen the separation, but again Wendy's mother surprised her. "And I miss you very much. Mrs. Kessler, let me check flight arrangements and call you back. It may be impossible to get any flights on Christmas Day."

"Evan and Wendy can meet you in Columbus or Cincinnati, whichever works better for you."

"I'll start checking flights right away and let you know," Emmalee said.

Wendy was slightly amused as she replaced the phone receiver. She figured the only reason Emmalee agreed to come was because she wanted to check out the Kesslers to see what kind of people *they* were before she agreed to her daughter's marriage into the family.

Three hours later, Emmalee called back to say that she would arrive at Columbus International Airport at noon on Christmas Day. Mixed with her apprehension over how Emmalee would get along with the Kesslers was Wendy's joy that she could be with Evan *and* her mother on Christmas Day.

Chapter Eleven

On Christmas Eve morning, Wendy helped Marcy and Olivia trim the tree. Wendy considered their finished result the ugliest tree she'd ever seen. Electric candles were hooked to the branches. They pinned individual puffs of popped corn to the end of the branches with straight pins because it was a German custom brought by the first Kesslers to Ohio. They wrapped yards of well-worn garland around the tree. Some ornaments had been made by Evan and his sisters out of clothespins and bits of fabric. They even hung some fragile paper ornaments made by Evan's grandmother.

In the family room, under Karl's watchful eye, Evan set up the smaller pine tree, which they adorned with strings of popcorn, pretzels and homemade cookies. After the tree was decorated, Marcy and Olivia placed the family's gifts beneath it—not even as many as was usually under the tree for Wendy and her mother. Other decorations collected by the family for years were placed in the central hallway, the parlor, the living room and the dining room.

"If you could make the stollen, it would be a big help to me," Hilda said to Wendy.

"I don't mind helping, but what is stollen? A dessert, meat dish, vegetable or what?"

"It's bread," Hilda told her. "A sweet bread, which can be used for dessert, or eaten with the main meal. We serve it for breakfast on Christmas morning."

Hilda handed Wendy a well-worn recipe card and took a large breadboard from a cabinet, putting it on the island in the middle of the kitchen. "You work here," she said. "This process takes several hours."

After reading the recipe over and over, and following Hilda's instructions, Wendy awkwardly measured out the dry ingredients and the spices, prepared the yeast and chopped raisins, currants and mixed candied fruits before she started mixing the batter. An hour later, Wendy had flour all over the countertop, on the floor, in her hair, on her face and all over her clothes, but she had the stollen dough ready to put in a bowl. With a sigh, she greased a bowl with shortening, put the dough inside and covered the bowl with a dish towel. She picked up the bowl and carried it to another cabinet near the stove where it would, hopefully, rise during the next two hours.

Wendy turned to survey the countertop and its collection of dirty cups, spoons and other utensils with displeasure. How could she possibly have used so many things to make a batch of bread that would yield only three loaves? By the time Wendy had washed all of the items she'd used, cleaned the flour off of the counter and floor, she was exhausted. And she wasn't even finished yet. Why would anyone go to so much work to make three loaves of bread when they could go to a deli and buy something equally as good?

I'll bet Kessler ancestors would have jumped at the chance to buy bread if it had been available to them, Wendy thought sourly.

Her temperament wasn't improved when Evan came in before she had an opportunity to tidy herself up.

He wiped her face with his handkerchief and kissed her cheek. "I couldn't find a clean place for my kiss," he said, his eyes alight with pleasure to see her participating in family customs.

She jerked away from him angrily. "I still have round two to go on my culinary work, so I can't see any reason to put on clean clothes."

"Aw, Wendy," he said contritely. "I was just joking."

"Well, I'm not in the mood for jokes." She turned from him and prepared the glaze she would need to spread on the finished product.

At the end of five hours, Wendy was not displeased with the looks of the bread. And since it was also traditional to eat some of the bread while it was still warm, Hilda asked Wendy to slice one loaf and give a portion to the family for an afternoon snack. The blend of cardamom and fruit in the tender warm buttered slice of bread was delicious, and Karl said, "You've…got the touch…for baking bread."

Wendy knew it was tasty, but despite his praise, she thought her time could have been put to better use than to have spent most of the day working on three loaves of bread.

While Wendy had been baking bread, Hilda had prepared the traditional Christmas Eve dinner of fresh sausage, baked apples and potatoes, a red cabbage salad and German plum cake for dessert. By the time the food was prepared, Marcy and Olivia had returned from delivering gift packages to their elderly neighbors.

When they sat down for dinner, Wendy had her first sense of belonging. She wondered if this was because she'd spent most of the day helping Hilda with the cooking. Evan put Karl in his wheelchair and brought him to the table. Karl asked the blessing on the food in his halting voice.

"God, we believe that one of your greatest blessings…is the gift of family. When you sent…the Lord Jesus to earth, You…placed Him in an earthly family. We believe…His early days at Nazareth, when…He was surrounded by loving family members, helped…prepare Him for the ministry You'd sent him to do. God, I thank You for…my family, the ones here at my table tonight, but…also those who've gone before me, and those yet to come. We pray…that Your Son will continue to live in…the hearts of this family. Thank You for…the food and the hands who prepared it. Amen."

After dinner, Evan insisted on putting away the left-over food, and he put the pans and dishes in the dishwasher. He wanted a little time to contemplate Wendy's reactions to the way they observed Christmas. He'd always thought that Wendy had missed so much because she didn't have a big family, and he had believed that she would eagerly embrace his family's traditions. Considcring her quietness and her solemn face during dinner, he didn't think she had.

After dinner, they opened the gifts under the tree in the family room. Wendy was touched that Hilda and Karl had included her in the gift-giving. They'd bought watches for Olivia and Marcy, a new cell phone for Evan and a set of matching earrings and bracelet for Wendy.

Some of the gifts were hilarious. Marcy's gift to Wendy was a picture of Evan on his first birthday, wearing only a diaper. Wendy apologized that she hadn't had time to make anything for them, but Marcy and Olivia seemed pleased with their earrings.

Wendy's fingers trembled as she opened Evan's gift, surprised to find an open-face antique silver chatelaine watch on a long chain nestled in a velvet-lined box. She lifted questioning, tearful eyes to Evan.

"It belonged to Grandmother Kessler," he said softly. "She willed it to me. I remember my grandmother wearing the watch. In the back of the case, there's a picture of me on my tenth birthday."

Overcome with a sudden comprehension of how much Evan loved her and how unworthy she felt to receive his love, Wendy leaned toward him. Ignoring his family, he pulled her into a tight embrace, kissing her tenderly. She withdrew from his arms, flushed and embarrassed.

"Thank you" was all she could say.

Wendy had debated long over a gift for Evan, but she'd finally written on a sheet of paper. "I promise to read a chapter in the Bible every day during the coming year."

The warmth in his eyes when he opened the envelope convinced her that she couldn't have chosen a better gift. They finished opening their gifts by ten o'clock. Gavin Kessler arrived soon afterward to stay with Karl, so Hilda could attend the Christmas Eve service.

Marcy drove her mother and Olivia to the church, but since Evan's grandparents had gone to the service in a horse-drawn sleigh, Evan wanted to take Wendy in the same manner. As hc hitched a fast-stepping horse to the sleigh, he wondered if he should have skipped this traditional event, since Wendy apparently wasn't overly impressed by what Kesslers of the past had done.

He helped Wendy into the sled and wrapped a blanket around her shoulders. He sat beside her and lifted the reins. They slipped out of the driveway at a rapid pace, because the horse was eager to go, but Evan restrained him. He hadn't driven the sleigh for years, and he wanted to get the feel of the rig. If the sleigh turned over, they could be badly hurt.

By the time they reached the secondary road leading to the church, their shoulders were covered with soft snowflakes. When thcy passed a neighbor's house, a light from the front porch shone on their faces. Glancing at Wendy, Evan saw that a faint light glowed in the depths of her dark eyes. Confident of his skill in driving the sleigh, Evan clicked the reins and the horse picked up speed. As the sleigh moved smoothly and quickly over the packed snow, Wendy squealed in delight.

"Hey, this is fun! Do you do this every year?"

"No. Most Christmases we don't have any snow."

"Then I'm lucky to have been here when it snowed."

That comment encouraged Evan, and his heart was lighter as he guided the horse into the parking lot of the church. It took a while for him to find a place among the automobiles to park the sleigh and tie the horse, which he covered with a blanket before they went inside.

It had been four years since Wendy had attended a church service, and that had been at a large church in Miami where her grandfather was the pastor, with a seating capacity of one thousand. Evan's church was a small building, and it probably didn't hold more than a hundred people, but every seat seemed full. A soloist's presentation of "Silent Night" greeted Evan and Wendy as their eyes adjusted to the dim light. Electricity hadn't been restored to the church as yet, so by candlelight they made their way up the aisle to where his family had saved a seat for them.

When the congregation stood to sing the opening carol, "Joy to the World," Evan and Wendy shared a hymnal. Wendy had heard the song often on television, but she wasn't accustomed to congregational singing, so she listened. She was amazed at the beauty of the music as the worshipers sang fervently, "'Joy to the world, the Lord is come; let earth receive her King.'"

An ensemble featuring a violin, a piano and a guitar played "O Little Town of Bethlehem." During this musical selection, Wendy recalled some of the words. "No ear may hear His coming, but, in this world of sin, where meek souls will receive Him still the dear Christ enters in."

One summer when she'd attended Vacation Bible School during a visit to her grandparents', all of the children were encouraged to memorize the sixteenth verse of the third chapter in the book of John. She had learned the verse, but had rarely thought of it since. Surprisingly, she hadn't forgotten the words. "For God so loved the world that He gave His only begotten Son, that whosoever believeth in Him should not perish, but have everlasting life."

Wendy imagined herself back in that church, hearing the minister as he'd given the invitation on the closing day of Bible school that year. Her heart had been touched, and she wanted to go forward and receive Jesus as her Savior. She'd closed her ears and her heart, knowing that Emmalee would be displeased because she had accepted her grandparents' beliefs rather than following her anti-church attitude.

But in this quiet place, with Evan holding her hand, she did what she'd wanted to do years ago. Her lips moved slightly as she quietly confirmed, "Lord Jesus, come into my heart." Wendy's pulse quickened, and she sensed a new spirit within her heart because she'd finally chosen God's way instead of her own.

After the sermon, the pastor extended an invitation for all believers to come to the altar to receive communion. Evan had decided that he would stay in the seat with Wendy, rather than to embarrass her and make her feel isolated. He stood so his mother and sisters could step into the aisle and join the line of people. Wendy stood, too. Hilda and her two daughters started up the aisle. With a smile over her shoulder at Evan, Wendy followed them.

"Hallelujah!" Evan whispered, perceiving he was

nearer the culmination of his dreams than he'd ever been before. Kneeling with the others, Wendy accepted a piece of bread from the hand of the minister's female assistant, ate it and took a cup of juice from the tray the minister held out to her.

Her heart filled to overflowing with praise and joy. Not only was Evan offering her a gift of his family, tonight she'd received another gift that had made her a part of the family of God.

When all the people had been served, the minister encouraged his parishioners to greet each other as they left the building. The ensemble pealed out the sounds of "Go tell it on the mountain that Jesus Christ is born," while the worshipers shook hands, hugged and rejoiced. Evan swept Wendy into his arms and whispered in her ear, "I love you."

The bell in the steeple was ringing, its mellow tones resounding through the hills when Evan and Wendy exited the church, holding hands. Evan helped Wendy into the sleigh, tucked the robe around her and hitched the horse to the sleigh. He sat beside her and locked her in a tight embrace.

"Evan, I can't explain what happened tonight, but I feel like a different person."

"You'll never be the same again. You've joined the greatest family on earth—the family of God."

"I'm kinda afraid, though," she said as he released her. "I feel a whole new life beckoning to me, and I don't have a map to guide my way."

"The Bible will be your guide into this new life. And

I'm going to be right beside you, giving you any help you need." His kiss was slow and gentle, but Wendy knew that his lips sealed the promise he'd made.

Chapter Twelve

As Evan turned the horse toward home, Wendy told him of her spiritual rebirth. "Just think, after all of these years, I still remembered the first time I experienced the call to follow Jesus. Do you think I've had that desire ever since then?"

"Probably. God is patient, and He's been gently pursuing you all of these years. You've made me very happy tonight. Will you let me share it with my family? They'll be overjoyed, too."

"I don't know. This is all so new. Let's wait until after Christmas."

"Since you took communion, they probably already suspect, but we don't have to talk about it tonight. We need to go to sleep anyway. One of our workers will do the milking tomorrow, so we can leave no later than eight o'clock to meet your mother in Columbus. Do you have an alarm clock or should I tap on your door when I get up?"

"I didn't bring a clock with me, so you'd better knock, please."

He left her at her bedroom door, and Wendy hurriedly changed into her nightclothes and got into bed, but she wasn't sleepy. To realize that she'd been rejecting God's call for years gave her an empty feeling inside. If she'd been a Christian, she might have had an influence over her mother. At least, she would have had the right spirit to have understood her mother's unhappiness. After an hour of soul-searching, Wendy knew that if she could live her life over, she would do many things differently. But she was only twenty-two, so surely she would have many years to serve the Lord. Her acceptance of Jesus had removed one barrier from her marriage to Evan, but she still had to determine if she could deal with the large Kessler family and their traditions. She figured seeing them en masse tomorrow would help her make a decision.

They made the drive to the airport in Hilda's car. Evan was aware of Wendy's nervousness while they waited for her mother. And he was a little edgy, too. Things were beginning to look favorable for their future engagement, but what if Emmalee put a stop to it? He sensed that Wendy was still not free from her mother's domination.

He didn't know what he expected, but Evan was surprised in Emmalee Kenworth. She was dressed impeccably, and was young looking.

Wendy waved to her mother as she came through the skyway door, and holding Evan's hand she hurried to meet her.

"Hello, Mother. Your plane was right on time. This is Evan."

Evan stepped forward to greet the woman, whom he hoped to make his mother-in-law. He shook hands with Emmalee, took her carry-on bag and stifled his surprise at the lack of a physical greeting between Emmalee and Wendy.

"It's nice of you to come to meet me on Christmas Day," Emmalee said. "I hope I didn't take you away from the family dinner."

To Wendy's relief, her mother was using the attitude she always showed to her customers, which had won her many sales bonuses and promotions. She'd sometimes wondered if having to be nice to customers all day wasn't the reason her mother was often grouchy at home.

"No," Evan said. "We had our traditional Christmas Eve dinner last night. Tonight is when our extended family joins us. We'll be home in time for that."

Wendy and Evan had eaten a snack while they waited for the plane. Emmalee said that she'd had lunch in Atlanta, so they left for Heritage Farm as soon as Emmalee's luggage was unloaded. Emmalee continued to be pleasant as they traveled, and Wendy prayed that her present behavior would survive the Kessler throng.

Vehicles were parked all over the property when they arrived at the house, but Evan carefully squeezed the car into the garage.

"I know you'd rather freshen up a bit before you meet the whole family," Evan said to Emmalee. "Wendy, take her up the back stairs to her room. We won't eat for an hour, so take your time."

"All right. Olivia is sharing Marcy's room during Mother's visit, so we'll have adjoining rooms. This way," she said, guiding her mother through the vacant family room and up a narrow flight of stairs that was seldom used. "We won't be long," she said to Evan.

A half hour later, Wendy wondered if Emmalee shared her apprehension as they walked down the wide stairway into the central hall. Emmalee had changed into a white silk ankle-length party dress. Long black pearls graced her slender throat and ears, and only an expert could have known that they were imitation pearls. She had repaired her makeup expertly before they left the room. Beside her, wearing a polyester pants suit, Wendy felt dowdy, but she was pleased that her mother looked so lovely.

Karl had been wheeled into the vast living room, and either Marcy or Olivia stayed at his side throughout the evening to meet his every need. Hilda took Emmalee under her wing, and Wendy marveled at her mother's glowing reception to all the attention she was receiving.

Wendy cringed against Evan when he led her through the crowded rooms that held more than a hundred people. She shook dozens of hands and was hugged warmly by strangers, hearing over and over, "Any friend of Evan's is a friend of mine." It was overwhelming to Wendy that anyone could have so many relatives.

When it was time for Hilda to supervise the serving of the vast amount of food that she and the guests had provided, Hilda asked Gavin Kessler to look after Emmalee. The two of them seemed to bond immediately, and they spent the rest of the evening together.

When the clock in the parlor struck midnight, Christmas was over for the Kesslers. Karl had long since gone to his bed in the family room, so the family departed as quietly as they could. Wendy stood on the front porch with Evan and his family waving goodbye to the guests as they drove away from the house.

Gavin was the last to leave, and he said to Emmalee, "I'll drive over tomorrow and take you for a tour of the county, if you like."

"I'd like that very much," Emmalee said. "I only have two days before I return to Florida, and I want to see as much of the area as possible."

Evan was standing close beside Wendy, and he nudged her in the ribs with his elbow. She had been watching Gavin and Emmalee with a dazed expression, and when she looked at Evan, he winked at her.

"Whew!" Emmalee said when they went to their rooms. "Wasn't that a terrible racket? I've never been around so many happy people."

"Neither have I. The Kesslers have been very good to me, but sometimes I'm overwhelmed by their closeness."

"I like Evan very much."

Wendy felt her face growing warm. "So do I."

"Have you made any plans?"

"Not really. We haven't talked about our broken engagement since I arrived. I still don't know if I can be successful as a farmer's wife, especially in the Kessler family. I had no idea how much work goes into operating a farm. Someday this house and farm will be Evan's, and when I think of following in Hilda's footsteps, I'm not sure I can do it."

"I have no objections if you do decide to marry. And I'm sorry that I haven't been a better mother. Being here with the Kesslers tonight has shown me what a poor home life I've given you."

Wendy hardly knew what to say, since she, too, had compared her childhood with Evan's more than once.

"I was really happy when Hilda invited you to visit. I felt bad about leaving you alone at Christmas."

"I've been scared to death ever since you left, fearing I'd lost you," Emmalee said, and tears filled her eyes. "Please forgive me for being such a terrible mother."

Wendy moved to her mother, and for the first time in many years felt her mother's arms embrace her. "I haven't been the best daughter in the world, either. Maybe this can be a new beginning for us."

"I realized tonight that I've wasted too many years being bitter about the past."

"And I want you to know," Wendy started, "that last night at the Christmas Eve service, I accepted Jesus as my Lord and Savior. In the days I've been with the Kesslers, I've realized that's what makes them such a unique family. If I put my Christian faith into practice like they do, I'll be a better daughter."

"You're not the one who needs to change, Wendy. I have to find it in my heart to forgive your father, and until I do that I'll never be able to have any happiness."

"I *would* like to have better communications with my grandparents and my father. In the past two weeks, I've seen how wonderful a family can be."

"Oh, by the way," Emmalee said. "Evan's uncle Gavin is coming to Florida in a few weeks, and he's asked if he can come and see me and take me out to dinner. I told him that he could. He seems like a very good man."

Well! So much for Gavin's intention to take me out to dinner, Wendy thought humorously.

"That sounds great," Wendy said, adding mischievously, "If Evan asks me to marry him again, maybe we can have a double wedding."

Emmalee playfully tapped Wendy on the shoulder. "Oh, stop your foolish talk." Then she laughed slightly, paused and said in wonder, "He's the first man I've been interested in since my divorce! I thought my emotions were so cold that I'd never feel anything again. Seems I'm wrong."

Sensing that she was on the threshold of a new relationship with her mother, after Wendy got into bed and turned out the light, she wondered what the future held for Evan and her. If he asked her to marry him, how would she answer? She thought about the reasons she loved Evan.

His good looks were what had attracted her in the beginning, but she'd soon learned that there was more to Evan than his handsome exterior. He was conscientious about his schoolwork. When she went out with him, he treated her like a queen. He opened doors for her, seated her at the table, always putting her wishes before his.

His solicitous behavior reminded her of the legendary Sir Galahad. Evan had made her feel loved and special long before he'd proposed to her. And she was convinced now that his family's influence had made Evan into the man she loved and wanted to marry. Although there were many things about the farm that chafed her, Wendy wanted her children to grow up in an environment that the Kessler family could provide.

Gavin came the next morning to have late breakfast with the family. When he escorted Emmalee to his car for the promised tour of the countryside, she was glowing and excited.

Evan said to Wendy, "I'm going to check on some stock this morning. Want to go with me?"

"Sure. How are we going? Foot, sleigh, tractor or…?"

He laughed. "By pickup, so you won't have to wear your coveralls."

While Wendy hurried upstairs for her coat and boots, Evan backed his pickup out of the garage. Victor came running and jumped into the bed of the truck. Evan whistled and motioned to Victor. The dog left the back of the truck, and with head down, tail between his legs, his belly almost on the ground, he crept toward the barn.

"Come here," Evan said, and Victor made a quick turn and galloped to Evan, who knelt down and put his arms around the dog's neck.

"This is a party for two, old buddy, and you aren't invited. Next time, you can go."

Victor was reassured by the tone of Evan's voice, and he walked to the back door of the house. When Wendy came out, the dog pushed through the open door, and Evan knew the warmth of the fireplace would compensate for the lack of a ride in the truck.

They were soon on their way, and Evan said, "I believe we have a new romance budding under our very eyes."

"You mean, your uncle Gavin and my mother? No doubt about it. I have never seen her so vibrant and happy. She admitted to me last night that Gavin is the first man she's been interested in since she and my dad divorced."

"Actually, this trip to check on the cattle is just a ruse to get you alone. I love my family, but they can get in the way when I want to court my girl."

He drove away from the homestead and turned on a road toward the hills, driving a short distance to the small house he'd shown her once before. He stopped and helped Wendy out of the pickup. "I brought the key this time, so we can go inside."

They walked up on the front porch, and while Evan unlocked the door, Wendy looked around. She could see the family home several miles away.

A breath of warm air greeted them, and Wendy said, "It feels mighty warm for a vacant house."

"I came here yesterday morning and turned up the thermostat."

The screened-in porch led into one large great room, and the focal point of the room was the stone hearth, fireplace and mantel. To the right of the cozy living area, a wooden island marked a kitchen and dining area, with cabinets of pine and a tiled floor.

Wendy looked around the room with delight. "This is like a dollhouse, Evan."

"My grandfather put brick veneer on the house when he lived here, but the original structure was made of logs. Daddy and Mom modernized the place during the years they lived here."

Evan directed her attention to a master bedroom, large bath and a smaller bedroom located behind the great room.

"There are two more bedrooms and a bath upstairs," he said.

"This is too nice a place to be vacant," Wendy said as Evan sat on the couch and pulled her beside him. He was as nervous as a teenager, trying to think of the right words to use.

"As I told you the other day, this house was the first dwelling built on Heritage Farm. It's been customary for the oldest son and his family to live here until they go to the big house. Mom and Dad moved here when they were married. My sisters and I grew up here."

Wendy was breathless, knowing what was coming.

"So you've seen the Kesslers at their best and the farm at its worst. I'm asking you again to marry me, Wendy, and move into *this* house with me. I told you last week that you'd be marrying me, not my family, but that isn't exactly true. You've seen how it is. I can't forsake my family when they need me, but I want you to become a part of that family. I love you so very much."

Wendy's heart danced with excitement. Her pulse quickened at the thought of living here as Evan's wife.

"Yes, Evan, I want to marry you. But you should

know that I'll never be able to fill Hilda's shoes, and I really don't want to. I love your family, and while I think their traditions are important, I'd like to put my stamp on the family. I want to be myself, not just another Hilda, doing everything just the way your ancestors have done. If we move here, I'd want to redecorate the house to my taste, even if it does change something your grandmother or mother had chosen. Do we have to live in the past? Why can't we start some traditions of our own? Do you understand what I mean?"

"Of course, and I agree with you," Evan said, amazed at Wendy's perspective, because she'd never shown such an independent spirit before. "You should finish your college and teach school like you want to do. God willing, it will be many years before we'll have to move into the big house. Once we're married, you'll be first in my life. If you don't want to live here, we'll live elsewhere, although I still feel obligated to help out until Daddy is better."

"I'd love to live in *this* house with you," Wendy said. "But I want to live here because we choose to, not because it's traditional. I'd feel like a prisoner if I knew the next fifty years of my life are already mapped out just because I marry a Kessler. And if my son wants to be an astronaut, or whatever, rather than a farmer, he should have the right to choose."

Laughing, Evan squeezed her until she gasped. "If you give me a son," he said, "he can be what he wants to be. And if our daughter wants to run the farm, she can."

"You do understand that I may end up doing everything just like Hilda does, but only because I want to."

"That's fine with me. And I've saved the best for last. A representative of Ohio State University contacted me a few days ago and asked me to consider taking a position as the county extension agent in this area."

Wendy experienced a sinking feeling. Was this something else to keep Evan and her apart?

"I wouldn't give him an answer until I had time to discuss the job with you."

"What kind of work would you do?"

"I'd be advising farmers and promoting agriculture in this area, with time left to still supervise the farm as much as Daddy wants me to. I have a cousin who'll take over the dairy work so I can go back to Florida this semester and finish the work on my Ph.D., while you're completing your work. We can be married in the spring, if you're willing."

His words released any doubt she had about marrying Evan. Flinging herself into his arms, before their lips met, she whispered, "I'm willing."

Evan released her reluctantly. He reached in his pocket and took out a box. With wondering eyes, Wendy opened the box and stared at the "past, present, future" ring she'd admired at the jewelry store the day Evan had proposed to her. The large diamond in the center and the two smaller stones on each side glittered in the shaft of sunlight beaming through the window.

"Oh, Evan!" she whispered. "This is the ring I liked best, but how did you know? Where did you buy it?"

"Before I left Florida last month, I swung by the jewelry store and bought it."

Wendy experienced a glow of pride that Evan, who'd

been worrying about his father, had taken time to buy a ring he knew she liked. She'd never again fear that Evan loved his family more than he did her. She snuggled close to him.

"I love you *and* your family, Evan."

Evan's thoughts turned toward the day when they would live in the ancestral home—his birthright—that they and their children would share during the years to come. He slipped the ring on Wendy's finger, sealing the promise of their future.

* * * * *

CHILD IN A MANGER

Dana Corbit

* * *

To my sister, Sabrina Puckett, my protector when I needed
one, my defender whether I deserved it or not, my fan
when I was insecure and always, always, my friend.
Special thanks to Laura Gentry, family case manager
supervisor for the Hancock County (Indiana) Division
of Family and Children for lending her expertise
and a small dose of reality to my fanciful tale.

And this will be a sign for you:
you will find the babe wrapped in
swaddling clothes and lying in a manger.
—*Luke* 2:12

Chapter One

The scenery couldn't have been more perfect if a wondrous star had appeared like a spotlight over the stable. Okay, a miracle or two couldn't hurt. Allison Hensley grinned at the thought as she stepped outside the New Hope Church building, the rumble of the crowd's competing conversations assailing her.

She inhaled the frigid December air, tinged with the competing sour-sweet scents of livestock and hay. Her breath spread before her in a moist cloud. When the wind picked up, she shivered, already losing the relief from the cast's indoor break.

Miracles. If she'd prayed for one this special night of Destiny's first, and hopefully annual, interfaith live nativity scene, she would have asked for balmy Bethlehem temperatures instead of this east-central Indiana chill. Local meteorologists were calling this weather unseasonably warm, but they weren't outside without gloves and dressed in costumes as thin as bedsheets, either.

Chin up, Allison. She rubbed her hands together and adjusted the shawl over her hair. She would just have to pretend she wasn't miserable and that her costume was fleece-lined. Maybe she should suggest that her best friend do a little acting of his own, outside his role as Joseph. David Wright was the picture of misery, scratching behind his beard where the adhesive must have itched, and shivering as he fidgeted with the belt on his robe.

"What's so funny, Mary?" David frowned. "Your pregnant belly is falling out, by the way."

Allison's hands lowered to the pillow beneath her robe, and she shoved it back where she guessed a growing baby belonged. "Thanks, Joseph."

A twinge of sadness fluttered over her that she probably would never cradle her own child in her arms, but she tucked the thought in the back of her mind where it belonged. She focused instead on her fellow performer, who finally had released his belt and had moved on to fussing with his strange hat.

"Quit fidgeting, or the audience will think Joseph has a tick."

"Well, thanks." Still, he dropped his hands and stared across the church lawn at the nearly two hundred spectators crouched in lawn chairs and huddled on blankets. "Why did I let you talk me into this? Just because you planned the whole thing didn't mean you had to rope me into it."

Allison grinned at David, eight years younger and the brother she'd never had. "You needed a new hobby, and the single women of Destiny needed a night off."

"At least one of us is going on dates."

Allison stuck out her tongue at him. It wasn't as if

guys were beating down the door to ask her out. Or that they ever had been, even earlier than five years ago when her thirtieth birthday had come and gone. "You won't change my mind. I'm not letting the ladies from the county assessor's office set me up with some new guy."

She hated feeling like an old-maid charity case. Besides, if she went out with the city's newest-ergo-most eligible bachelor, she would be a cradle robber, too. Busybodies in town were always thorough, so Allison already knew the bachelor in question was just in his early thirties.

"You never know...."

Yes, she did. A lifetime of being the chunky girl whom boys chose for a pal instead of girlfriend had taught her plenty about too-high expectations.

"You can forget it. I'm not going."

David opened his mouth to say something else, but one of the local farmers approached, leading an old Shetland pony—the show's version of a donkey. Instead of saying whatever he'd planned to before, David gestured toward the "donkey." "Ready for the long journey to Bethlehem?"

"Ready if you are."

After a quick ride across the lawn for effect, and an unfruitful visit with the innkeeper, they stepped inside the stable for the rest of the performance. As silence settled over the crowd, a musician started strumming chords on an acoustic guitar.

"'Away in a manger, no crib for a bed...'" the choir sang, the significance of those well-known lyrics seeming to join the spectators in a singular mind-set of worship.

Allison could have sworn that the stars shone brighter for just a few seconds. The moment was perfect. It was poignant. It was spiritual.

Until the doll in the manger started to cry.

Brock Chandler didn't know exactly when the crime had been committed, but he did recognize the moment his night off had ended. Not when the kid started wailing. Instead, his job started the moment the woman portraying Mary gasped and raced over to the manger, dropping her pillow stomach on the way. So much for his plan to relax in the back of the audience and get to know his new community by watching one of its folksy events.

Like a round of "the wave" in a football stadium, audience members leapt to their feet by rows.

"The baby's real!"

That someone announced the obvious with as much shock as an alien sighting telegraphed that the rest of the audience had been expecting a plastic doll Baby Jesus wrapped in those swaddling clothes. And, from the chaos in the stable, so had the cast.

Shaking off the irritation that a hectic holiday weekend for the Cox County Sheriff's Department had just become busier, Brock pushed his way to the rustic stage and through the human wall of cast members, heavy blankets now draped over their shoulders. But when he reached the inner circle, the hay-lined trough was empty, and the Mary character was soothing the baby in her arms.

Brock drew in a breath and stared. Mania surrounded her, and yet the woman holding the child appeared serene. At home even.

When he'd initially seen her riding her make-believe donkey into the fictional Bethlehem, he would have described her as more cute than pretty. Her face was slightly wider than oval-shaped, and her nose was pert rather than elegant. But as she cradled the baby, her hazel eyes shone with emotion in the stage lights, and her full lips turned up in a sweet smile that transformed cute into lovely. Like some small reflection of the Madonna she'd portrayed in the stable stage.

With extra care, the woman pulled back blankets to reveal a red-faced infant in a thick, hooded bunting. As she loosened the hood, she traced her fingertips along a tiny cheek.

Something strange and warm unfolded inside Brock's chest—so out of place for a law-enforcement officer. Too soft, those feelings were unacceptable for him, on or off the job. As unacceptable as any form of weakness. Rubbing his gloved hands together, he stepped closer to the woman.

"Excuse me, folks. I'm Sheriff's Deputy Brock Chandler." He didn't miss how everyone glanced at his leather jacket and jeans where his uniform should have been, or the way the woman's head jerked at his introduction. One day he'd get used to the strange reactions some people had to police officers, but it hadn't happened yet.

As was his habit, Brock ignored the woman and searched for a man who could provide details. His gaze landed on the Joseph character. "Can you explain the circumstances involving this infant?"

But the woman stepped in front of her fellow performer. "We're not sure who left this little one, or even whether it's an abandonment or a practical joke." She scanned the chattering crowd with a hopeful expression, as if expecting the child's mother to rush up and reclaim him.

Brock didn't have to look at the crowd. He knew the broad—make that the suspect—wasn't coming back. Deserting mothers never did. And this woman on stage was naive if she believed differently. After several seconds, she turned back to him, her disappointment obvious in her frown.

He flipped up his jacket collar to cover his freezing ears while ignoring the temptation to regret the woman's loss of idealism. His own had died a long time ago, and good riddance to it.

"Well, I don't see anyone rushing forward yelling 'Gotcha,' so we'll investigate this as a crime. But first we need to phone an ambulance and child welfare concerning the abandoned child."

"That won't be necessary," the woman whispered, staring down at the infant who'd finally fallen asleep.

"Excuse me?" His harsh tone caused the child to startle, so he lowered his voice. "What are you saying?"

"You won't need to call child welfare. I'm Allison Hensley, an FCM—that's a family case manager—for the Cox County Division of Family and Children. It's part of the Indiana Family and Social Services Administration."

Brock opened his mouth to respond, but the woman had the gall to turn away from him to speak to the Joseph character instead.

"David, could you get my cell phone and call the ambulance? My bag's behind those hay bales."

Then she walked over to the Wise Men. "Hey, guys, could you do some crowd control? We need a path up to the stable for the paramedics to get through."

Only after she'd succeeded at removing all of his authority in the situation did Allison return to stand in front of him.

"Okay, now let's—"

Brock raised a hand to interrupt her. *Let's?* She might have stepped in the middle of his first worthwhile investigation in terminally dull Destiny that by luck rather than population had been made Cox County's county seat, but there would be no *us* in the rest of his case.

"Way to be on top of the child welfare thing," Brock said, loud enough for only her to hear. "Talk about being at the right place at the right time."

It had to have been the caustic tone he'd attached to the last comment that had her raising an eyebrow at him. "I believe God puts us where He needs us to be."

"Tell that to your Baby Jesus there. Did God plan for his mother to dump him like a bucket of slop in that hay trough?"

Sure, Brock believed and all, but it was awfully hard not to question God's will and even His strength in a world where children were left to fend for themselves.

The social worker pulled the blanket closer around herself and the child as if shielding them both from his harsh words and the truth they reflected. Then she shook her head. "I don't know."

"Well, I think this mess was the plan of a woman with major baby baggage and a flair for the dramatic. Perfect stage to dump a kid, don't you think?"

"*I think* we don't have any idea how desperate the mother's situation is. There are only two things on my mind right now—having this child medically evaluated and finding him temporary shelter." She glared at Brock. "This baby is the only thing that matters."

"Except finding the perp who dropped him here." He used the TV cop slang for *perpetrator* to annoy her, though he wouldn't have been caught dead using the term at the sheriff's department. "That's *my* job."

"You're not the only one with a job to do here. And it would help mine, too, if the mother would reappear this instant, but until then, I have to fill out a 310—an intake report—and get this child to the E.R."

With that she turned away from him again and yanked that veil thing off her head to reveal a long ponytail of dark blond hair.

His back teeth ached from grinding as he turned to the Wise Men. "Who was watching the stable in the last twenty minutes before the show?"

The tallest of the trio filled Brock in about the cast's break and suggested crew members who might have crossed the set during that time. The others explained how the manger initially was hidden by hay bales so the audience wouldn't see Baby Jesus.

"Where is that doll, by the way?"

But the cast didn't have to respond because David rushed back, holding up the doll and a bulky diaper bag.

"Look what I found. Baby Jesus was on top of this bag, and it was right next to your duffel bag."

Allison flashed Brock a knowing glance, as if the vinyl diaper bag with puppies printed all over it vindicated her forgiving opinion of the mother. "She wanted us to find that stuff."

"Like she wanted us to find her baby," David supplied.

"Wait," Brock called out, but it was too late. David was already rifling through the bag, digging out diapers, formula, bottles and some of those sleeper-jumpsuit things. So much for lifting any clear fingerprints.

David held up one of the bottles. "Look, the formula's already made up." As the baby started fussing, he stepped over and coaxed a pacifier into his mouth.

Brock shook his head. No wonder the two of them had played the lead roles in the nativity scene. They certainly were a pie-in-the-sky pair who saw the best in people when Brock had so often glimpsed the worst. Pair? Were they? He studied them a few seconds more, their connection obvious as they comforted the child together.

That he was even curious only annoyed him further. *Are you here to investigate a crime or to pick up women?* Especially one who dressed as Jesus' mother in her spare time. And was exasperating and likely already taken. Didn't he ever learn? Between his birth mother and Robin, he would have thought he'd survived enough lessons for a lifetime, but obviously he craved more punishment.

Relief flooded him as ambulance sirens blared in the distance, signaling the caseworker's departure and his chance to regain control. Soon Allison and her charge were in the ambulance, heading to Cox County Hospital, and he could finally properly investigate the crime scene.

He focused on the details, looking for anything out of place in the stable, besides stage lights and a Shetland pony. Chances were the mother wasn't far away, and he was determined to find her and arrest her. A child had been deserted today. No, he wouldn't allow himself to think of another abandonment long ago or to mourn on this child's behalf. He didn't have time for that. This situation was different than the other. This time, he could do something about it.

Chapter Two

That this particular infant lowly had turned out to be a *she* instead of a *he* was just one more surprise in a long evening of them. But Allison was too anxious to appreciate the irony of it. How could she when she needed to place a child only hours before Christmas Eve?

Inside that barred hospital crib that opened on the side like an animal's cage, the snoozing baby—whom the staff had already deemed "Joy" because of her holiday arrival—appeared even tinier. More pitiful, though the staff pediatrician had deemed her healthy.

A lump clogged Allison's throat, and her nose burned. To escape the moment's intensity, she stepped outside the room to the bank of pay phones she'd visited several times since their arrival two hours before. But the disinfectant smell and the child's image trailed after her, both clawing their way inside her mind and body.

Joy. She tested the name on her tongue. The name fit, and at least it was more personal than "Baby Doe." The baby was alone in the world, like so many of the other children Allison helped in her work. Precious gifts from God, these little ones had been neglected, abandoned or abused by the very parents He'd entrusted with their care.

Joy's mother was as guilty as the rest. Allison wouldn't even have defended the woman if not for her instinctive need to shield her gender against that infuriating deputy's criticism. Clearly, the guy had issues with women.

Didn't the sheriff's department question job candidates about whether they had problems with people of different races, religions or genders? Someone had neglected to ask Brock Chandler. She wondered what would make a man like him—one who'd been blessed with dark brown, wavy hair and deep blue eyes—hate women when he'd probably always had his choice of them. Had the effortless successes made him feel disdain for the prizes?

She shook her head over that. Reclaiming her thoughts from their odd tangent, she dialed the phone, contacting her department director for an update. She didn't have time to worry about other people's problems when she had a sizable one of her own in the form of that tiny arrival.

"Clara, it's Allison again." She spoke into the receiver. "Joy—I mean the infant—is fine. We're just waiting to hear on some blood work."

"How's the search coming?" In the background, Clara Johnson's own children could be heard wreaking havoc. A deep male voice kept calling for them to settle down.

Knots multiplied inside Allison's stomach. "No luck

yet. I've left messages with most of the foster parents on the list. Doesn't anyone stay home for Christmas anymore?"

"Except for you and me, I'm thinking no. Wait. Hold on." Clara covered the phone, probably for some choice words with her family, before speaking again. "Did you contact Superior II yet?"

"No, I was waiting…just a little while…hoping—"

"Have you forgotten state law says you've only got forty-eight hours after taking a child into custody before a hearing to determine if she's a CHINS?"

She hadn't forgotten. But did it hurt to hope for a few hours that the mother would reappear with a family member who planned to take custody of the baby? Especially at Christmastime. She couldn't be wrong to hope that Joy could avoid becoming part of the system as a Child in Need of Services. Naive, maybe, but not wrong.

"Allison, are you still there?"

"I'm here."

"It's getting hectic here. Call me when you know more. And contact the court."

As she was hanging up, Allison heard footsteps stop behind her. She turned to see the one person who could make a difficult night worse. Still dressed in jeans, a chambray shirt, leather jacket and cowboy boots, he looked more appropriately dressed for a date than an investigation. Or a *GQ* cover shoot.

Judging by the outdoorsy cologne that drifted from him, she guessed it had been a date, probably with some lucky, thin twenty-year-old. A man like him—someone who turned heads when he walked through a door and, once inside a room, exuded masculinity to its four walls—never had to settle for any woman past her twenties or anyone, like her, who would have to have two surgical plates implanted to have buns of steel.

"Deputy Chandler, is it?"

Okay, she knew that was his name, but she couldn't think of anything better to say, and he wasn't exactly jumping at the chance to speak first.

He nodded, and if she wasn't sure she was mistaken, she would have thought he shifted uncomfortably. But he straightened again. "I didn't recognize you without your costume."

Then it was her turn to be uncomfortable as she glanced down at her oversize sweats and wished she hadn't changed. The robe would have masked her many figure flaws.

She folded her arms over her chest, wishing the action would shield the rest of her body from view. "My friend David—you know, Joseph—brought me some clothes to change into."

His only response was an affirmative grunt followed by silence that stretched too long.

Her chest tight, Allison resisted the temptation to fuss with her ponytail, which by now had to have morphed into a rat's-nest style. There wasn't a thing she could do about her stark complexion since she'd scrubbed off that orange stage makeup in the hospital rest room an hour before.

She waited for disgust to appear in his eyes at the dumpy picture she must have presented, but his focus was on her notebook with its half-crossed-off list of names. He didn't seem to notice her at all. Which was worse. Shame filled her that it mattered what he thought.

He shifted his gaze back to her. "Oh, I'm here to check on the infant's status. Were there signs of abuse?"

At the same time, a nurse, one of Allison's high school classmates, passed by them. "How's our little Joy? Is she sleeping?"

"Yes, finally. It's been a tough night for her."

Brock was staring at her, his eyebrows drawn together, when Allison turned back to him. "Joy? She?"

She nodded. "The baby's a girl. She's about four weeks old, according to the pediatrician. Healthy, too. She eats like a horse." Allison grinned at the memory of holding the baby while she inhaled an eight-ounce bottle. "Some of the staff have started calling her 'Joy.'"

"So they think abandonment is a cause for celebration?"

She resisted the temptation to snap back at him. "The doctor also said she shows no signs of physical abuse."

"The woman's Mother of the Year, right?"

Holding her breath seemed to be the only way to keep from hollering, "What's your problem?" Why was he baiting her? Did he expect her to be the defender of women everywhere? It was as bad as an unbeliever expecting her to speak on behalf of and defend the not always Christ-like actions of all Christians.

When she could trust herself to speak civilly again, she answered, "I doubt she'd win any trophies."

You wouldn't win, either, if we're talking about compassionate police work, she was tempted to add. She changed the subject instead. "How is the investigation going so far? Are *you* closer to locating her?" She couldn't resist putting extra emphasis on *you* though she felt guilty for her inability to turn the other cheek.

"We have half a dozen witnesses."

When Allison jerked her head to meet his gaze, he wore a gloating expression. Again she held back, refusing to let the arrogant deputy get to her. Nor would she allow herself to see how blue his eyes were, like an ocean at night and just as mysterious. She couldn't remember anyone who'd ever agitated—or intrigued—her more. Neither of her reactions to him was acceptable.

"That's good. What did they have to say?"

Brock seemed to ponder for a minute, as if deciding whether she could be trusted with investigative information. "They all described a short, lumpy-looking woman hanging around the stable," he said finally. "She wore a long hooded coat that easily could have hidden a baby. The witnesses said she wasn't a local."

"You can trust them on that one. Destiny only has a population of seven hundred, you know."

"I work here, remember?"

"For only two months or so." It was *exactly* eight weeks since Brock had started at the sheriff's department, and she knew it. How could she not know with as much noise as the local busybodies had made over the new bachelor's arrival? But she wasn't about to let him know that. Her cheeks burned, so she studied her notebook, hoping he wouldn't notice her blushing.

"Long enough," he said.

She had to smile at that. He would never be in Destiny long enough to truly be a part of the place. Only coming into and exiting the world within a ten-mile radius of town made that possible. "Did anyone see her later?"

Brock shook his head. "Apparently, she didn't stick around for the stage show."

Rather than remind him that he'd assumed the mother would have enjoyed watching the chaos on stage, Allison made an affirmative sound in her throat and pushed on the door to the E.R. patient room. "Want to go in?"

Reluctant couldn't begin to describe his expression or rigid stance with hands jammed into his jeans pockets. Still, she sensed him following behind her as she stepped into the room, his nearness disturbing.

A glance back at him halted her step and muted her negative thoughts about members of the county's finest. The man who had appeared stingy with his empathy, was frozen near the doorway, unable to take his eyes off the sleeping child. In the same way, Allison couldn't stop watching him.

Finally, he inched toward the cagelike crib, his gaze never leaving its occupant until he gripped its vertical bars. This vulnerability, so incongruent with his all-male swagger, was strangely appealing. Even with his jaw tightened, Brock's face still appeared more boyish than chiseled, more Dennis Quaid than Arnold Schwarzenegger. She doubted he would appreciate the observation.

Whatever battle he waged ended as he slipped a hand between the bars and traced his fingers over Joy's cap of light brown hair. He touched her gently, as if she were formed of blown glass and he couldn't risk crushing her.

The image stole Allison's breath. It made her wish for things she ought not to wish for. To daydream when it was too late for such nonsense. At this moment it didn't seem such a stretch to think of her own child resting comfortably in his daddy's arms or to imagine someone she loved touching her own hair with such reverence.

The baby startled in her sleep but settled back to her dreams. Still, Brock pulled back his hand just as Allison reclaimed control of her thoughts. Who was she to question God's will? She was certain God planned for her to remain single so she could be the most help to forgotten children. For many of those lost in the system, she was all they had. And right now, she was tiny Joy's only hope.

"You know," she whispered, "I need to get back to these calls before she wakes up." Allison indicated her notebook that held only a few remaining possibilities.

Brock turned to face her and nodded, moving toward the door, his tight posture relaxing with each step away from the child. "I've got work to do, too." He lifted the diaper bag from the chair and carried it into the hallway.

With a glance at the still-sleeping baby, she followed him out. "I'm going to need that."

"I keep thinking there's something that we've missed—something that will lead us to her." He set the bag on the ground and kneeled next to it, digging inside.

"We've already gone through it. The only things in it are diapers, formula and stuff—the necessities."

Brock only shook his head and kept digging, piling the contents on the chair. "There's got to be something."

But there wasn't. He reached the bottom and searched the pockets, finding only baby products and clothing. The sleepers and blankets were new and clean, but they were common items, probably available at any discount department store.

He grunted his frustration and stuffed everything back in the bag. "I'd better get back to the department. I have to check on the report from all the area hospitals and follow up on other leads."

Allison nodded. Of course, the sheriff's department would be checking up on women who had delivered recently at area hospitals. She did him the favor of not asking him about his leads when they both knew he didn't have many.

"Good night, then." He jutted out his hand in what appeared to have been an automatic gesture, and just as instinctively, Allison grasped it.

The moment he closed his fingers over hers, his grip strong, his hand massive enough to make even hers seem small, she recognized her mistake. She should never have touched him. Her arm positively thrummed from elbow to wrist, and he'd only touched her hand.

Maybe because he'd felt it, too, or more likely because she'd clutched too long, he yanked his hand away. With an awkward wave, he turned and left. The click of his booted heels echoed down the corridor until he disappeared through the elevator door.

A disturbing emptiness settled over Allison, and she felt alone, despite the occasional nurse or medical technician passing by. *No, I'm not going to do this.* She was happy being alone. She was content. No way would she allow some stranger to pass through her field of vision and make her question God's plans. She couldn't afford to let herself wish for more or to wonder if she'd been wrong about what she believed He wanted.

But the questions overwhelmed her best efforts to avoid them. If God intended for her to marry, wouldn't He have given her some sign? If He had, would she have been watching closely enough to recognize it? And the biggest question of all—were the night's events the sign she was looking for?

Get a grip, will you? She shook her head, trying to do just that. A bunch of people had gone to a lot of trouble to be a part of this alleged sign of hers. The live nativity's cast and crew, representing all four of Destiny's churches. The crowd. Young Joy and her misguided mother. Brock Chandler.

She had no idea whether Brock was part of some elaborate sign or not, but she understood he was a huge distraction. One she could ill afford tonight when the baby inside that room needed her to be singularly focused on her welfare. Now that the handsome deputy was gone, she could get back to her job. And she could finally breathe normally again.

Chapter Three

Allison lowered the pay phone onto its cradle with a click as she studied the list of names again. Already she'd crossed all but the last one, so this time, with a heavy hand, she put a line through it. What was she supposed to do now?

From inside the room, she heard the first small whimpers that probably would escalate into newborn wails as Joy came awake. A peek at her watch told Allison it had been three hours since the baby's last bottle, and she was probably hungry, wet or soiled—or all three.

Instead of dropping coins in the pay phone again, she walked back into the room and lifted the phone on the bedside table as she opened the side door on the crib. Tucking the phone under her chin, she used both hands to lift Joy. Once resting against Allison's chest, the baby began rooting against her, obviously accustomed to nursing.

Allison only felt more useless as the child fussed and searched hopelessly for sustenance. She'd been unable to find temporary housing for the child, and now she couldn't even give her a mother's milk. She couldn't fulfill any of her needs. Lifting a pacifier from the bag, she slipped it between the child's lips and hoped it would sustain her a few minutes longer until she could ask the nurse for another bottle.

She dialed the phone with her free hand and started talking as soon as her boss answered. "Clara, I've been through all the names. I can't find anyone."

Clara strung together a few of those colorful words she was prone to using in stressful situations, and Allison tried not to listen, feeling just as frustrated.

"What are we going to do?" Allison used the word *we* even though it was really up to the department director. There had to be some advantages to not being a supervisor, outside the long hours and low pay that were the bane of a career in social work. "I have no options left."

The older woman was quiet for a several seconds before she spoke again. "Well, there is one."

"I've been over the full list of foster parents. There's no one."

"I know of someone."

"Are you listening to me? No one is available."

She wanted to reach through the telephone wire and shake her boss, who had become uncharacteristically dense in the past few hours. "If you have some other name, I need it now because the nurse is bringing the baby's release papers."

Clara cleared her throat. "I was talking about *you*."

Some Christmas Eve this had been, Brock thought as he trudged through the sheriff's department and dumped his notebook on his desk at dinnertime. If he weren't so cross-eyed exhausted from pulling an extra shift, he might have looked over his shoulder to see if the notebook had toppled his desk's mountain of chaos. But at this moment, he could only look straight ahead… to coffee.

The day had suffered from a lousy start, and it had gone downhill from there. Even the morning headline had read "What Child Is This?" as some clever headline writers had played on the words from the old Christmas carol.

If the weekly *Destiny Post,* best known for its no-longer-news content, had scored the scoop, then even the three or so people in town who missed last night's comedy of crèches and didn't have a direct link in the gossip chain knew about the abandoned baby. They also knew about his failure to apprehend the suspect. And it was only a matter of time until the Indianapolis networks descended on Destiny like ants on an uncovered brownie to report the cheesy Christmas story. No doubt they'd write a sidebar article on police incompetence over the response.

For the hundredth time today he wished the crime hadn't occurred in a public venue. But wishing did no more to change the facts than it did to make his cup of coffee taste less like tar smelled. He took a swig of the brew anyway and grabbed the stack of pink messages off his desk. He riffled through them, hoping at least one would provide the lead he hadn't found all day.

Contacting hospitals and shelters all the way from Greenfield to Kokomo hadn't produced a single, solid clue. But he was far too stubborn to let the case grow cold. Someone had to have seen the mother after the show, and he was determined to find that someone, even if he had to interrupt every Christmas celebration in town.

When he was on the next to last message, he shot a glance at the sheriff's dispatcher, Jane Richards, in her windowed office.

"How's it going, Chandler?" she asked, but turned back to her computer without even waiting for his answer.

"Dandy," he said anyway.

His coworker appeared annoyed at having to work while everyone else spent time with family, attending Christmas Eve services or roasting chestnuts, if people outside storybooks really did that. Too bad for her she had a family to go home to. On nights like this one, when law-enforcement officers worked double shifts while the rest of the world celebrated, it paid to be alone in the world. Just the way he wanted to be.

So why did a picture of that know-it-all caseworker appear in his thoughts like a neon sign blinking on and off with the word *liar?* And why had his apartment, perfectly sized for a bachelor who didn't put much stock in furniture or electronics or clothes or anything that took up space, seemed so tiny this morning? And empty?

The holidays were probably getting to him. No wonder suicide rates increased between Christmas and New Year's. Newspaper articles and commercials featuring Norman Rockwell holiday images were designed to make people like him wonder if they were missing something.

Did Allison Hensley ever worry she was missing anything? She was single and lived alone; he'd checked out that information himself earlier in the day. And she'd made a point of calling David Wright a friend; whether for his benefit, Brock wasn't sure.

Maybe she'd just been searching for something to say to cover up her discomfiture over the outfit she'd been wearing. He couldn't understand why the sweats had made her so uncomfortable. She'd looked fine. More than fine—even with her hair all messy like that. All soft and feminine and relaxed enough for a night of videos and popcorn. At least until he'd mentioned her costume.

Still, she wasn't the only one who'd been feeling discomfort in that hospital hallway. Otherwise, why would he have said some idiotic thing about not recognizing her? As if he wouldn't have known those intense, long-lashed hazel eyes, even if she were dressed in a pillowed pumpkin costume and had painted her face orange.

That reality bothered him far more than facing the sassy social worker at the hospital. Since when did he go around noticing women's eyes, even if this particular pair seemed to change at will between green and golden brown? And since when did he suffer from such a chemistry shock upon simply shaking a woman's hand? Well, no matter when it had started, it needed to stop right now. Unless those eyes—or hands—happened to belong to a particular deserting mother, and if he did touch her hands, it would only be to snap on her cuffs.

Joy. How ironic that someone had given that nickname to the baby. Joy was likely the one emotion this
child would never experience.

Shaking off the strange musings that he could at-
tribute only to a lack of sleep, he lowered his gaze to
the last two messages in his hand. The one on top was
a tip regarding his most crucial local case prior to this
one—a rash of power tools burglaries. As that case
would just have to wait, he flipped past it to the last
message.

His breath caught as he looked down at the same
name he'd been trying all day to forget. Allison Hensley. His palms started sweating before he'd even read
what she had to say. Her message was as surprising as
the fact that she'd called at all. She'd be providing temporary foster care for the infant? At her own home?

Brock didn't have to ask himself where he was going
as he gathered up his notebook and his jacket. And he
refused to ask himself why. He didn't even have to look
up her address again, since he'd already done that and
had passed by her small ranch home three times since
then, always on his way to somewhere else. And always
wondering if she had more interesting plans than his
for Christmas Eve.

Now he knew for certain that she did, but they
weren't the kind he'd imagined with a bit of jealousy
he had no right to feel.

Despite the misgivings forming a jumble of knots in
his gut, Brock hurried past the dispatcher and out into
the early-evening darkness. During the three-minute
ETA to her house, he would have to come up with some

plausible excuse for being there. But he didn't care. None of his valid reasons for staying away from her seemed to matter right now, even if he couldn't explain his attraction for the woman who dressed like Mary. He could tell himself he was only checking up on the abandoned infant, but truth be told, he was far more curious about the baby's temporary caregiver.

"What are you doing here?" Allison asked as she pulled the front door open, her expression a blend of shock and confusion. Her gaze followed his tan sheriff's department uniform from boots to service belt and weapon to hat.

She stood in the parquet entry, her damp hair hanging loose to her shoulders, bare toes peeking out from the flared bottoms of her jeans. Like the night before, she looked fresh-faced without makeup, and she appeared nervous again, this time pushing her hair behind her ears.

"I just came to—"

But from inside the white-painted house, an infant shrieked.

Allison grimaced. "I've got to get her." Already, she backed away from the door. "Come inside. I'll be right back." She turned and rushed down the hall.

All the calm he'd manufactured during the short drive in his sheriff's cruiser disappeared as he stepped inside. He shoved his hands in his pockets as much to wipe off his sweaty palms as to quit fidgeting. So much for the tough sheriff's deputy.

Inside, the house didn't seem to match the woman

he'd met. It didn't have the same vibrancy so apparent in her smile or the intensity that flowed from her pores. Brock took in the floral wallpaper and the antique furniture, crowded with bric-a-brac. Even on the Christmas tree in the corner, ornate glass ornaments were crammed on branches next to paper-and-glue angels and loads of tinsel.

When Allison didn't return for several minutes, he ambled over to a claw-footed curio cabinet, staring at the figurines stuffed inside.

"Those were my mother's. This was her house."

Brock startled at her words and turned to see Allison standing behind him, a sniffling baby resting against her shoulder. "Oh. They're nice."

She chuckled and started swaying to some tune that perhaps only she and the baby could hear. Though the infant had been in her care less than twenty-four hours, Allison moved with a practiced rhythm. Her face glowed.

"Not exactly my taste, but she loved them," she said, still talking about the figurines he'd already forgotten in favor of a much more interesting figure, this one dressed in faded jeans and a soft-looking red sweater.

Allison lowered her gaze to a bell collection on one of the dark wood end tables and smiled. "Mom and I never agreed on decorating, but since she died a year ago, I haven't had the heart to change anything."

"Sorry to hear that," he said.

Instantly, Allison's gaze cleared, and she turned back to him. "I must have forgotten. Lack of sleep will do that to you. Did you say why you're here?"

"Rough night?" As soon as he said the words, Brock regretted them. He had no business asking her questions about how she'd spent last night or any other. Especially with the kind of innuendo that she couldn't have missed.

A pleasant flush crept across her cheeks, but she didn't call him on it. "Our Joy has her nights and days mixed up. So we watched a lot of infomercials together last night. And in the morning."

As she spoke, Allison switched the wiggly infant to a reclining position, and immediately the child started rooting against her chest, so she lifted her back to her shoulder. "She's hungry."

"I can see that." Again, the words escaped before he could stop them. He'd seen that, all right. Now he could only watch her blush again. He had no business replaying the scene and wondering what it would be like to touch Allison himself. He had to either get control of his hormones or leave right away for both of their sakes. He chose control.

"I'm off-duty. I just stopped by to check on Joy." Funny how much more believable that statement had sounded when he'd practiced it in the car. And even more surprising, he'd called Baby Doe by that nickname that suddenly seemed appropriate for a child receiving Allison's care. If only every child were so privileged.

Allison stifled a yawn and nodded, as if she accepted his flimsy excuse for being there. "Well, I need to warm a bottle for her, and she's wet so—"

"Here, let me help." He stepped forward and lifted Joy, a new and disturbing experience. She was so tiny, squirming and pushing her head back as he rested her against his shoulder. He lifted his finger to the child's tiny hand, and her fingers curled around it as if she, too, realized they were connected in their losses.

As natural as anything he'd ever done, he brushed his lips across the baby's forehead. She smelled so much like Allison's light, floral perfume that he wondered what it would be like to kiss the woman herself.

When he looked up, Allison was staring at him, her expression so strange that he worried she'd read his inappropriate thoughts. But she turned away, leaving him oddly disappointed. "The stuff's in the diaper bag. Could you change her?"

"Sure." He was anything but, though he'd shoot his foot with his own sidearm before he admitted it. How hard could changing a diaper—only a wet one, thankfully—be? He crouched by the diaper bag and pulled out one of those changing pads he'd seen parents use and spread it on the floor before resting the baby on it.

As if she knew what awaited her, Joy started fussing. But he couldn't let that distract him as he studied how the diaper went on before he released the tabs that secured it. He was prepared to master this task—and impress Allison—if it killed him.

"Are you doing okay out there?" she called from the kitchen just as he had the wet diaper open.

"Sure we are—" he paused as he stared down at Joy's sore-looking backside "—except, is her bottom supposed to be this red?"

As if he'd just pointed out that the child was missing a limb, Allison rushed back into the living room carrying the bottle. She appeared as uncertain as he did as she studied the problem. "I think it's diaper rash." She set the bottle aside and started digging through the diaper bag. "I thought I saw a tube of cream in here."

"Yeah, I saw one, too." He reached over to dig with her, stilling his hand as it brushed hers. Their gazes caught and held in what felt like a timeless pause before she pulled her hand from the bag and looked away.

"It has to be in there somewhere," Brock said to cover the awkwardness. He grabbed the bag and dumped it on the floor, with everything, even the plastic-covered cardboard piece that stabilized the bag's bottom, falling out.

And he saw it.

Taped to the bottom of the cardboard piece was a white index card and the clue he should have found earlier. Written in block letters, the message was brief.

Sweetheart,
Remember that I love you.

Your Mother

His thoughts whirled and escaped to that forbidden place in his past. His fingers tingled with the memory of long wavy hair that a boy could touch. He fisted his hands to exorcise it. "Yeah, she loved her, all right. Enough to desert her."

Brock whispered the words, but he knew Allison had heard it because she glared at him as she dug in the bag's zippered pocket and produced the missing tube of cream. She elbowed him out of the way, applied a thin layer of the sticky white ointment and diapered the baby.

"This child's mother left her where she was certain to be found." She snapped the sleeper back into place. "She'd cared for her well. Even the doctor said so. And she wanted her child to know she was loved. Who are you to judge her? How can you possibly know her heart?"

"Oh, I know, all right, how easy it is for women like her to walk away. To cut those apron strings with a machete and never look back."

Allison jerked with shock the way he'd expected her to, but she said nothing as she washed and dried her hands at the sink. Then she turned back to him, leaning against the living room doorway. "Brock, are we talking about Joy's mother...or yours?"

Chapter Four

Brock's stark expression as he looked up from the note answered more succinctly than any words he could have spoken. But he put on a mask of disinterest in the same way he probably donned his brown uniform and assumed the air of authority that went with it. Allison didn't buy his act this time.

Those broad shoulders that had filled out his leather jacket the night before and earlier had straightened the seams in his uniform shirt now curled forward. As if one opponent in his life could still best him.

Avoiding the temptation to study him further, Allison reached for the bottle and offered it to Joy, who drank greedily. She smiled at the hearty appetite of a child blissfully unaware of the drastic turn her life had taken. That she'd become a statistic.

When Allison glanced up again, she caught Brock studying them. Her pulse fluttered even though she reasoned that he was only looking at her because she nestled a critical part of his investigation. The victim.

"The only mother we need to worry about right now is hers." He poked a finger through the air toward Joy.

Allison flinched and was glad the baby was so pre-occupied with her dinner and the bright color of her caregiver's sweater that she hadn't startled at Brock's sudden movement. At least he hadn't bothered to deny her guess about his own deserting mom because she wouldn't have believed him if he had. His anger was too palpable for him not to have scars of his own.

As he wasn't sharing any details and didn't appear likely to anytime soon, she switched tacks. "Are you going to have the note dusted for fingerprints?"

He shrugged. "I could, but I doubt it will produce any leads. The only way her prints would be in the NCIC—the National Crime Institute Computer—would be if she'd been booked for a crime."

"But you doubt that's the case, right?"

"She's probably not in there." Brock raised an eye-brow at her as if expecting her to gloat.

She only nodded. Why it was so critical that he not believe Joy's mother to be a criminal—at least prior to this—she wasn't sure. It could have been that she wanted affirmation of her willingness to give the mother the benefit of a doubt, but she wondered if she just wanted some proof that Brock Chandler wasn't en-tirely jaded. His belief in humanity was tarnished at best.

For a few seconds, she focused on Joy alone, who was nodding off after having inhaled half of her eight-ounce bottle. She sensed the deputy's gaze, warm upon them, and allowed herself a few minutes to enjoy the fantasy that she'd caught such a handsome man's attention.

His nearness was disconcerting, but she couldn't escape it because his presence filled the room. She wanted to believe it was the uniform, the badge, the gun at his hip that took up so much space, though she guessed it was much more likely the man himself.

If only she could have stayed as she was—secretly tickled by his attention—instead of becoming self-conscious. Had he noticed how large her thighs appeared in those jeans or how her long sweater masked a pesky ten pounds she never could seem to lose?

"Here, let me feed her." He took a step closer and stretched out his arms.

"Wait, I need to burp her first."

She glanced down at the child relying so completely on her. It surprised her to realize she didn't want to share Joy at all, even after the exhausting day she'd had. That was crazy. She had no business becoming attached, not when keeping a professional distance was essential to case management. They'd never been just cases to her, though. They were children. This particular child had come into her house, slept in her spare room in a portable crib and climbed into her heart.

Feeling Brock's gaze on her again, she lifted the baby to her shoulder and used the burping technique the nurse had demonstrated for her. Unfortunately, none of her patting or rubbing on the child's back did the trick.

The floor creaked and the room shrank again as Brock stepped in front of her. "Here, let me try that."

"Have you ever burped a baby before?"

"No, but that's not stopping *you*."

He settled the cloth diaper across his shoulder and lifted Joy from her arms, settling her against his shoulder and patting the child's back with his much larger hand.

Allison chuckled, the tension of moments before dissipating. "Hey, I've done this lots of times. Well, most of them in the past day or so, but I'm still pretty experienced at burping infants."

"That makes one of us."

But Joy chose that moment to release a particularly loud gas bubble. Brock looked over the top of the baby's head and smiled.

She couldn't help grinning back. "Two now."

As if he'd done it a million times, Brock deftly switched the baby back to a reclining position and held out a hand for Allison to pass him the bottle.

"She'll get less gas if you hold her head up higher."

Instead of questioning her limited child care expertise, he shifted Joy higher and popped the nipple between her lips. The baby happily accepted her dinner as Brock settled on the sofa to feed her.

Allison couldn't help watching him. A gentle giant, Brock seemed to envelop Joy in khaki as he held her with such care. He couldn't seem to take his eyes off the baby or stop from running his fingers through her fuzzy hair. Did he have any idea what a contradiction he presented? Such a tender heart buried beneath that steel exterior. He would probably think of that as weakness when she only saw strength. His heart had survived much, and still, no matter what he wanted everyone to believe, dared to hope.

Brock traced his fingertips along the baby's jaw, and Joy turned her face toward the sensation. Allison could almost feel his touch on her own cheek. If only she too, could be the recipient of Brock's tender ministrations.

Now you're jealous of a baby. That's just piti-ful. Maybe she'd bought into the local matchmakers' schemes more than she'd realized. She'd even convinced herself that Brock had been watching her when it couldn't have been more clear that his whole focus was on Joy...where it should have been. Where her own priority should have been if she'd had her head on straight today.

"She doesn't eat like a poor, mistreated foundling, does she?"

"Is that what you were?"

He looked away long enough that she guessed he wouldn't answer, and then he did. "I guess I was, but my story isn't as glamorous as Joy's."

"Most of them aren't."

"Let's just say that, like Joy, I had a mother who couldn't be bothered to raise me. But unlike her, I was older—five—when Madeline hit the road. I remember."

He stopped then and glanced at her sharply, as if he resented revealing so much about himself, when he hadn't said enough as far as she was concerned. She suddenly needed to hear it all—about the injured little boy he'd once been, how he had overcome his pain, what led him to a career in law enforcement. Her heart ached over what little she knew and so much she didn't know.

From his expression, though, she guessed he wouldn't be telling her any more about himself, at least not today.

"I'm sorry, Brock."

He made a noncommittal sound in his throat and looked away. When he glanced back at her again, that stark expression had vanished from his eyes. "It doesn't matter. I really lucked out anyway, having Roy and Clara as my adoptive parents." He paused for a few seconds and then changed the subject. "So what's the next step for the Division of Family and Children?"

Allison stiffened. Obviously, Brock was right. Their focus couldn't be on him or anything else when Joy needed them so much. Time was running out for her to avoid becoming part of the system.

"I've already completed the 310, and I'm working on the 311," she said. "That's the investigative report we use to substantiate or unsubstantiate abuse or neglect."

"That sounds a lot like an arrest report."

"It is, only the type of detention is different."

Allison responded to his surprised look by raising her shoulder and letting it drop.

"I've waited as long as I can for the detention hearing, but it's going to have to be tomorrow to make the forty-eight-hour deadline."

"Why did you wait?" But the sides of his mouth pulled up, and he didn't wait for her answer. "You thought she'd come back, didn't you?"

"Hoped." She waited for him to berate her for her belief in people who maybe were undeserving, but he didn't. It was just as well because even she had to admit that her hope was running out.

Instead, he stood, his sudden movement startling Joy enough that she released the nipple and whimpered.

"This little girl needs us to do something besides sit around and hope." His voice was strange, hard, as he handed the baby into Allison's arms.

As she slipped the bottle back in the baby's mouth, she swayed in a rhythm that had soothed Joy several times before, but this time she wouldn't accept the bottle and refused to be comforted. How could Allison expect to calm the infant when she was so rattled herself?

Obviously, Brock was as frustrated as she was that they'd been unable to locate the baby's mother, but that didn't give him any right to take it out on her.

"I'm not sitting. I'm doing everything I can right now." But the way Joy continued to fuss made her wonder if it would ever be enough. This poor, sweet child deserved more than she could give. "And I'll get her placed with one of our foster families just as soon as I can."

"You're not the only one with a job to do."

His arms crossed over his chest, Brock glanced down at the coffee table where that index card and his only new clue lay looking so impersonal with its block letters.

"Nothing's ever going to be okay for her until her deserting mother is behind bars." He whispered, but the vehemence behind the words made up for the volume.

He didn't even have to say he planned to be the one to lock that jail cell door. As if he could right the world's wrongs—past and present—by wielding a set of handcuff keys. Who did he think he was, Dirty Harry? She was pretty sure that kind of vigilante justice wouldn't go over well in Destiny, and he needed to know it, too.

"How is locking up her mother going to make things right for Joy?" The minute she said it, she was sorry, but it was too late to take it back and to behave like the Christian woman she should have been. The woman she had so much difficulty being when the deputy was around.

Brock's posture tightened for a few seconds, and then he let his shoulders fall with defeat. "Maybe it won't make things right. Maybe it's too late and nothing can."

"You don't believe that, do you?"

Even as she asked it, she knew that he did. Again she wondered if he was talking about Joy or himself. "No matter how bad our troubles are, God can make it right. Or at least He'll help us to bear the load."

Allison braced herself, expecting him to ridicule her again about her faith, but he only nodded as if he wanted to believe, too. For Joy's sake, if nothing else.

She understood the helplessness he must have felt when trying to do right by Joy. She'd experienced similar feelings so many times at work—when the courts still returned children to birthparents who'd worn out too many second chances, when a child fell through the cracks. Would Joy slip through, as well, leaving Allison, her hand reaching and clasping only the thin air of futility?

Brock shrugged. "The only thing we can do is do our jobs. It's been a long day—" He paused long enough to glance first at the baby, who was finally drifting off to sleep, and then at Allison's face "—for all of us."

"Tomorrow might be even longer." She yawned, exhaustion descending on her. Her evening with night owl Joy would likely be a long one. "Well, Christmas is in a few hours, so Merry Christmas."

One side of his mouth pulled up in a sad half smile. "Happy holidays to you, too."

Allison smiled at the irony as Brock let himself out the front door. She carried Joy to the portable crib. There was nothing merry about this Christmas Eve, nothing happy about an infant who had to begin her life as someone's castoff, or a man who still couldn't get over having been deserted the same way.

Yet, imperfect as it was, Allison could still recognize the gift in this last night before Christmas. The sleeping child in the crib made her believe in God's promises. She had a child to cherish tonight, even if that joy was only temporary. But there was more to it, she decided, as she crossed back into the living room, suddenly so empty despite her mother's furnishings.

All throughout Destiny, families were probably together, enjoying each other's company and loving or hating carefully chosen Christmas gifts. So why did she get the strange feeling that the best gift she could ever hope to receive had just walked out her door?

Christmas Day dawned gray and frigid, the ground a dreary brown without the blanket of snow many of Destiny's children had probably mentioned in their bedtime prayers. Brock didn't even want to ask himself what he was doing back at Allison's house that morning because he wasn't in the mood for self-incrimination.

Standing on her front steps, his hand poised to knock, he hesitated. The wrapped gifts in the shopping bag that dangled from his other arm suddenly seemed like bad ideas. Coming here again was the worst idea of all. Last night his excuse of checking on Baby Doe's status was almost believable. Less than ten hours later, it didn't have that same credible ring to it.

Brock backed down a step and lowered his hand. It wasn't like him to waffle after he'd made a decision, but this situation didn't fall under the realm of "ordinary," either. His best—and safest—choice would be to get back to the sheriff's department and focus on the investigation the way he should have been. He couldn't afford to let his guard down. He'd done that one time with Robin, and look where that had gotten him.

So why did he continue standing there like some sweaty-palmed teenager, certain he didn't want to leave and yet unable to bring himself to knock? Sure, he wanted to see the baby again. That was part of why he was here—trying to make up for some of what she'd lost.

But he was only fooling himself if he didn't admit that most of his attraction for the house with the gaudy furnishings had to do with the hazel-eyed blonde caring for that baby. As much as he hated to admit it, his heart had betrayed him as he watched her lovingly tend to that defenseless child, tempting him to wish. For what? Someone to care for him? He was a big boy; he couldn't rely on anyone. Relying would mean trusting, and that was just impossible.

Still, something about that woman drew him to her.

She made him crazy and fascinated him at the same time. The world she envisioned was so different than the one he knew. She saw scalable mountains where he found brick walls. Her belief in humankind was so unshakable that she still believed Joy's mother might return. While at first he'd ridiculed her Pollyanna attitude, he suddenly envied her optimism and was enchanted by the light that surrounded her.

He glanced down once more at his bag of presents. This was Christmas. It wasn't presumptuous to give gifts today. Merely polite. He might have had a lot of faults, but bad manners wasn't one of them. Before he changed his mind again, he raised his hand and knocked.

Chapter Five

Allison stumbled to the door, clasping Joy in the same loving football hold she'd used several times during the night. So many times, that if the baby were truly a stitched leather ball, Allison figured she should have scored a few touchdowns by now. But even mind-numbing exhaustion wasn't enough to stop her pulse from dancing when she saw Brock through the glass side panel in the door.

She had to be reasonable. He was probably here because of some break in the case or even to take one more look at that diaper bag to see if it had produced another new clue since last night. She pulled open the door, managing to keep from patting down her morning hair. By now, Brock probably thought her regular look was either a biblical character's robe, sloppy sweats or baggy jeans.

"Merry Christmas, Allison."

He gave a smile that would have made a lesser woman swoon as his form filled the entry. Out of uniform, he looked fresh-shaven and handsome in a cream cable sweater and tan slacks. The skin on her neck felt warm, and it had nothing to do with the cheery fire from the gas log in the fireplace. She could barely take her eyes off Brock to study the bag of gifts at his feet.

"Christmas? It's morning already?" she said, stifling a yawn.

"Joy kept you awake again?"

Even her smile felt tired. "She was too excited to sleep, I guess. So she needed me to keep her company."

"Looks like she's catching a few z's now." He slipped past her into the living room and stood next to the Christmas tree before turning back to her.

Allison lowered her gaze to the sleeping baby for a few seconds before returning her attention to Brock and his bag of surprises.

His gaze followed hers. "I didn't see any presents here last night, so…" He let his words trail off, indicating with a tilt of his head the bag by his foot.

"I've already mailed my sister, Heather, and her husband theirs. And I cheated and opened theirs to me when it came in the mail."

"I can see you as a gift snooper." He grinned. "Sure glad I didn't bring any over last night, or you might not have been able to resist the temptation."

She studied his face, trying to understand his meaning. All the gifts weren't for the baby? She'd seen the way Brock had looked at Joy last night, so it didn't surprise her that he wanted to indulge the sweet, helpless baby on Christmas. But she was taken aback that he had remembered her, as well.

Holding up a finger for her to wait, he rustled through

the bag and set several messily wrapped gifts under the tree. Then he produced a small wrapped gift the size of a thin book and made a big production of bowing over it and extending it to her. "For you."

"You didn't have to." On the other hand, she was tickled pink that he had, and she couldn't help letting him know it with her grin.

"It wouldn't have been any fun if I'd had to."

"I'm sorry. I don't have anything for you." *Anything you'd want, anyway.*

One side of his mouth pulled up in a silly half grin, but still he stepped closer. Her heart humiliated her by tripping again as if she expected him to give her a Christmas kiss to go along with the gift. She wasn't convinced she could deny him if that were his intention. Brock only reached toward her arms, though, and lifted Joy.

"Here, I'll hold her while you open it."

Unlike her temptation the night before to cling to Joy, keeping her only to herself, today she welcomed the opportunity to share the child's care with Brock. Relief filled her as she delivered Joy into his capable hands. She didn't need the gifts he'd brought to convince her that the baby had captured his heart as effectively as she'd snatched Allison's. But the fact that he'd taken the time to purchase and wrap last-minute gifts just so the foundling wouldn't be forgotten on Christmas Day tunneled inside her heart.

That he might have made the gesture to salve his own childhood wounds didn't lessen its impact. Joy would never remember the rattles or teething toys inside those packages. She would forget her mother. Allison only wished Brock could have been as fortunate with his own.

"Aren't you going to open it?"

"Oh…yeah." Resisting the temptation to tear into the holly-design wrapping paper, she carefully slid her fingers along the seams. Gifts were rare treats for her these days since her mother was gone, so she planned to enjoy this one.

"You're one of those, aren't you?" he said, indicating her hands with a movement of his head. "Are you going to carefully fold under the tape so you can reuse the paper?"

Allison paused before she'd uncovered her gift. "If I were more ecologically responsible, I'd try that, but it would mean having to find a place to store all that extra paper, and I hate clutter."

Brock peered from one side of the living room to the other, his gaze taking a leisurely journey over collections of pewter animals, ceramic teacups and silk flower arrangements. Too many of each.

When he faced her again and grinned, Allison couldn't help smiling back.

"Remember, this stuff was my mom's."

"None of it's yours?"

She shook her head, though technically all of Mary Hensley's treasures now belonged to Allison and her older sister, Heather, who as yet hadn't collected her share. "I'm in some of the pictures in the hall." But even those weren't really hers, just the collection of a doting mother.

He crossed to the corner of the living room where Allison had placed the loaner car seat she'd used to bring Joy home from the hospital. Carefully, so as not to wake her, Brock settled the baby into the seat, taking the receiving blanket from the coffee table to tuck around her.

Then he stepped back to Allison and pointed to the gift she still hadn't unwrapped. "Now you'll have something else that's yours."

Allison released the last strip of tape to reveal a silver picture frame. "Oh, it's lovely. Thank you."

She rolled the frame, an appropriate gift for an acquaintance, around in her fingers. The metal felt cool, smooth in some places and rough where a trail of flowers had been etched into its surface.

"How did you manage to find something so beautiful on Christmas Eve?" Instantly, she was sorry she'd asked. It made no difference where he'd come up with the present on such short notice—even if he'd re-gifted it.

But he only chuckled at her question. "Don't rub that frame too much or the plating might fall off. If you're willing to drive about fifty miles and shop shoulder to shoulder with other procrastinators, you can find gifts on Christmas Eve, but you might have to sacrifice quality."

"Don't you put down my present." She wagged her index finger at him and then hugged the frame to her chest. "I happen to love it."

"I'm glad."

His gaze was mesmerizing. She couldn't have looked

away if she wanted to, and right now she had no incli-
nation to try. Not when this was the most perfect holiday she could ever remember.

Finally able to pull her gaze from his, Allison
stepped to the sofa and indicated with a gesture of her
hand for Brock to join her. She sensed his nearness before she felt the cushion shift under his weight. Still,
she stared into the flames in the fireplace, allowing its
melding of reds and yellows to calm her shaky nerves.

Brock sighed. "This is nice. I bet the fireplace in-
sert was your idea."

"It was. How did you know?"

"It seemed more like you than…the other things."

"I had it put in when Mom was really sick. She liked
to stay warm near the fireplace."

Brock cleared his throat. "I'm sorry about your
mother."

"Thanks. She's at peace now." Again, she waited for
him to criticize her beliefs the way he had at the live
nativity, but he didn't.

"I'm sure she is," he said finally.

So he did believe, after all, even if his belief system
was a little jaded.

"Are you still in contact with your father?"

"He passed away when Heather and I were still in
high school. Mom never got over losing him."

"She was lucky to have you with her."

Allison smiled at that. For a few minutes longer, she
stared into the fire, relishing the silence and the company. She didn't even realize she'd started humming

until Brock joined in with her and started singing softly with a surprising bass voice.

"'Joy to the world, the Lord is come...'"

They finished the hymn together then softly continued singing carols of Bethlehem's blessing, of a child in a manger, of *excelsis Deo*. Allison relaxed into the sofa cushions, contentment making her extremities deliciously numb. She'd imagined Christmas mornings like this before, not with sleigh rides and painted scenes but with the warmth of family as they celebrated together God's wonderful gift to a dark world. With the loving husband and children she'd tried so hard not to wish for anymore.

Okay, she'd hardly imagined an abandoned infant and a disillusioned deputy in her dreams, but this was nice, too. Precious. She lowered her gaze to the frame resting on the end table. Brock probably assumed she would place a picture from her personal life inside the frame. She wondered if he realized that moments from last night and this morning were more poignant than most of the others she could tuck behind that glass.

"You know," Brock began, his voice soft as he broke the silence, "I think Joy is going to sleep away the whole holiday." He chuckled. "And after she was too excited to sleep last night waiting for it."

Allison motioned with her hand toward the Christmas tree. "Do you think we should open her presents for her?"

"Absolutely." Brock rubbed his hands together in childlike excitement and popped up from the couch.

"Who goes first? Age before beauty?"

Brock drew his eyebrows together. "I know which one of us is better looking, but I don't know who's older."

"That would be me. I'm thirty-five."

"Oh, I'm thirty," he said, proving the matchmakers had their information right. "I guess that means I won't get to take a turn."

She'd expected shock over her advanced age, but it didn't seem to matter to him. "Wow, a gentleman— that's a rare find these days."

Their gazes caught, held, for what felt like hours in the passing of seconds. The surface of her skin tingled beneath his stare. The way he looked at her made her long to touch, to hold, to cherish. Were those things possible in her life?

A rare find. Brock was certainly that for so many reasons. For his humor, his strength and for the giving heart he'd tried his best to hide, but couldn't.

Surely, before too long someone else would *find* Brock. Someone younger, prettier and with more to offer than she. The slice of pain in her belly gave a hint of the ache she would feel when that happened.

For her self-preservation, Allison finally looked away from him and kneeled by the tree, collecting a large, awkward-shaped package. She shook it next to her ear.

"I bet it's a toy."

"Wow, you must have X-ray vision."

"Just me and the other superheroes." This time she ripped into the package. A standing activity gym with dangling toys emerged from the wrapping paper.

"Think she'll like it?"

Allison grinned. "I know she will. I sure do."

She liked everything about today, most of all having Brock here, close enough so that she could see the ocean in his eyes, smell his pine tree-scented soap and feel the timbre of his laughter inside her own chest. Her gaze caught on his smile, on his thin lips and slightly crowded teeth, and she wondered what it would be like to kiss him. Uneasy, she stared at her grasped hands. How pitiful of her it was to wish for impossible things.

Brock opened the next present himself—a police car. "I know she won't be able to play with it for a long time, but I couldn't resist."

The symbolism in the gift tugged at her heart. Was he trying to let Joy know that someone did care about her and wanted to protect her? Of course, he could just have selected it because it was a cool cop toy, but she sensed there was more to it than that.

Allison had just reached under the tree for the next gift, which squeaked as she grasped it, when the telephone rang. For several seconds and two more rings, she only stared at the phone.

"Are you going to answer it?" Brock asked, cocking his head.

She nodded, trying not to feel the disappointment already flitting on the edges of her happiness, as she moved to the phone and lifted the handset. Who was on the line didn't matter because the call had already interrupted the moment, had brought them slamming back to reality.

No matter how much she wished it otherwise, this

Christmas-morning family was only in her imagination. Brock wasn't her husband. Joy wasn't her child. And her Cinderella moment, when she could pretend to be whomever she wanted, to have whatever she chose, had passed.

She could no longer pretend she was someone with endless possibilities. She worried, though, that she would never be satisfied with her life again.

Brock didn't need Allison to reveal who was on the phone, when watching her told him all he needed to know. Her expression fell. Breath seemed to whoosh from her lungs. Then her gaze shot over to the baby, who lay there wide-eyed, having awakened with the ringing phone.

"Oh, Margaret, I'm so glad to hear you're back in town....Merry Christmas to you, too....I have a four-week-old female infant to place....Yes, the abandoned child in the newspaper... Oh, you saw it on TV?" She paused in her telephone conversation and frowned at Brock before continuing. "You'll be able to take her? That's great."

Her carefully blank features and her curled shoulders as she looped the phone cord around her fingers suggested the situation was anything but great. His own gaze drifted to Joy, who was glancing about at her newfound world. Soon Allison was planning details about delivering Joy to the foster parent named Margaret.

Without taking the time to dissect his gut response, Brock moved to the car seat and gathered the baby into his arms. He didn't want her going anywhere but where she was. She was safe here with Allison…and with him.

Okay, buddy, you're losing it now. He'd lost his edge. What was he doing there, enjoying the holly and the ivy and playacting downright domesticity, when he needed to be out there finding this child's birth mother?

He rested the baby against his shoulder. As if to prove her strength, Joy pushed her head back and stared up at him. He couldn't let her down. No, wouldn't. She didn't need his failure to add to that of the most important person in her life.

Brock glanced at Allison as she lowered the phone back to its cradle. She looked so tired, lavender half-moons of exhaustion suddenly apparent under her eyes. Until now, she'd been wearing her lack of sleep well, her contentment easily masking it.

"I guess you heard," she said when she stood close enough to brush back the baby's sweaty hair.

"You've done your job. I need to do mine."

She nodded, but he could see the sadness in her eyes. He needed to believe that her distress was over having to deliver the baby, not his leaving. She'd be making a huge mistake if she started to rely on him. If she did, that might tempt him to put his trust in her. That was something he just couldn't do.

Chapter Six

Allison's eyes burned as she descended the foster home's front steps. Her feet felt so heavy. Her hands... empty. So many times before she had left children in the loving care of foster parents, but it was different this time. It felt as if she'd left a part of herself with the bundled child and her stack of Christmas toys.

She couldn't say Joy wasn't in good hands. As soon as Allison had walked through the door, Margaret Ross had relieved her of the infant car seat, unbuckled its precious cargo and gathered the baby to her bosom. Her husband, Bob, appeared next to her and ruffled Joy's dark hair. Soon teenagers—the Rosses' biological and foster children—swarmed the living room to meet the new arrival.

There was plenty of love to go around in the Ross household, enough to share with an abandoned child. Too bad none of the warmth Allison felt there could go with her as she walked out into the gray Christmas afternoon.

In her car, she switched on the radio but kept flipping through stations as all seemed to have dedicated their December 25 playlists to holiday music. That only reminded her of singing carols earlier with Brock, of sensing his nearness at she watched flames shimmying in the fireplace, of sharing Joy's first Christmas. Finally, she just shut off the radio.

Her dark mood followed her as she returned to her house, too quiet without the sound of a baby crying for her next bottle or Brock's deep, rich laughter. An emptiness enveloped her that even the twinkling Christmas tree lights couldn't penetrate. The empty silver picture frame that before had offered such promise only mocked her.

Maybe to torture herself further, she trudged down the hall to the room she'd always thought of only as "Mom's room," at least until Joy had slept there. The portable crib still sat in the corner. All of it—the picture frame, the deserted crib, even the empty space beneath the tree—reminded her of the life and the family she would never have. She'd never missed the unknown so much before.

But it wouldn't do her any good to think about that now. Restless energy had her packing the portable crib into its case and collecting the remaining blankets to take to the Rosses' when they met for the court hearing that night at seven o'clock. She'd stalled as long as she could, but they were running out of time.

When everything was packed away, she returned to the kitchen and started capping bottles in the drying rack by the sink. As she dried the last, she noticed the blinking light on the kitchen phone for the first time. How long ago had someone called? Was it Brock? She shook her head, determined to think sensibly. The call could have come from anyone—David, another friend, her boss or a representative of the court. Her sister could even have called. It wasn't unthinkable on Christmas Day.

But despite her plan to be sensible, her pulse raced when she read "Cox Co. Sheriff" on the caller ID box. She held her breath as she hit the answering machine button. A female voice came on, asking if she could collect some gifts left at the department offices for Baby Doe.

For the first time since she'd left Joy with the Rosses, she smiled. She shouldn't have been surprised that the people of Destiny were reaching out to the foundling, especially since Joy had become something of a holiday celebrity around town.

So many times Allison had resented her community's outpouring of support for the less fortunate at Christmas because those efforts assumed that people weren't hungry, lonely or suffering any other time of the year. Tonight, though, she sensed her friends' compassion as they reached out to Joy, just as she and Brock had. She wished Joy could grow up in Destiny and have the opportunity to be enveloped in such warmth.

She glanced at the tree again. It looked so lonely without that pile of gifts, as lonely as she felt in the house where she'd been mostly content until today. If not content, then settled. She was neither now.

If only she had accepted one of the many invitations from friends to share Christmas dinner so she didn't have to stay home. Her gaze shot back to the answering machine light that was no longer blinking. Well, there was one place she could be. Someone needed to pick up those gifts from the sheriff's department.

She wouldn't be going just to see Brock. Nor was the possibility of seeing him the reason for her getting ready for a shower and laying out her new red sweater with the bell cuffs and her favorite black slacks. She just wanted to get some wear out of the sweater, a Christmas gift from her sister, and red was a good color for the holiday.

She was just coming out of the shower when the phone rang again.

"Have yourself a merry little Christmas," her best friend's crooning voice filtered from the receiver.

"Merry Christmas to you, too, David. Why are you calling me? Is the dating schedule a little slow?"

David made a wounded sound into the phone and then laughed. "You know full well I'm suffering through the traditional Wright family Christmas gala. But speaking of social calendars, how's our Deputy Chandler?"

Allison swallowed hard and wished she hadn't talked about Brock last night when David had called. She'd convinced herself it had only been a casual mention, but David had this annoying habit of seeing through her.

"He brought the baby some presents this morning." She didn't mention the gift Brock had brought for her, but she smiled over her secret.

"Oh, am I interrupting?"

"He isn't here. Neither is Joy."

"You placed her?"

Allison made an affirmative sound in her throat though her heart squeezed.

"Then you're free for Christmas dinner, aren't you?"

Getting out of her friend's invitation while sidestepping his questions took some fancy footwork, but she managed it while keeping most of her dignity.

Within minutes after hanging up, she stood with damp hair before the mirror, applying eyeliner and mascara that she usually skipped and reminding herself that Brock probably wouldn't even be at the office. He would be out on patrol or following up leads on the investigation.

But if their paths did happen to cross while she was there, then at least he would finally get to see her looking her best. Even the small prospect of seeing him again that day made her Christmas merry after all.

Just after noon, Brock gripped the edge of his desk so tightly that his fingertips turned red while his knuckles flashed white. Okay, it didn't feel as freeing as punching a wall would have, but it did take the edge off the stress mounting inside him. He released the desk and rubbed his fists against his gritty eyes. Something had to cut through the tension if he was going to be able to take a fresh look at the investigative report.

Maybe he needed another blaring wake-up call like the one this morning to help him get his head on straight. That call from the foster parent had reminded him that, Christmas Day or not, it was time for him to get back to this investigation, even if the trail had gone colder than the temperature outside.

He'd sure needed some kind of wake-up call at Allison's, something to awaken him from the domestic way he'd sat there with her. Since when did he go around singing Christmas carols, anyway? But he didn't really have to ask, remembering well the music that was alive in Roy and Clara Chandler's living room.

Just thinking about this morning's cozy scene made him feel warm, as if he could still feel the heat of the fire's glow on his face. He could even smell the floral scent of Allison's shampoo as it had imprinted on his senses.

No wonder he couldn't come up with any new ideas for the case when his thoughts kept flitting back to her. Instead of feeling guilty over being distracted, all he could think about was finding a different excuse to see Allison now that she was no longer caring for Joy.

He would have continued to berate himself the way he deserved if the object of his distraction hadn't stepped through the glass door to the receptionist desk. She didn't look like herself with her hair all twisted and tied up off her neck, her face made up and fancy clothes and a long dress coat in the place of her comfortable things. He couldn't take his eyes off her, but he couldn't decide if it was because he preferred this glamorous version of her or if he couldn't get over how she'd messed up a good thing.

"Excuse me, you're Jane Richards, aren't you?" Allison asked the dispatcher. "I'm Allison Hensley."

The woman laughed. "I know who you are. I was in your mom's book club."

Brock pretended not to notice how Allison conducted a conversation with the dispatcher but appeared to be studying him instead. Her cheeks became like twin berries when he nodded at her.

Jane glanced back and forth between the two of them and quirked an eyebrow. "I take it you've already met Deputy Chandler."

"Several times," Brock answered.

Allison nodded and rolled her lips inward, smudging all that lipstick she wore.

The older woman cleared her throat. "Hey, you made a great Mary the other night."

"Thanks," Allison answered. "The night didn't quite go as we planned."

"The world's like that, isn't it?" Jane chuckled. "Well, people have been dropping by gifts to Destiny's own child in a manger, but from the size of these boxes I'd say it's other stuff besides gold, frankincense and myrrh."

Allison turned to stare at the stack of gifts in the corner, her eyes going wide. "Thank you for contacting me. I'll take everything to her foster family when I meet them at the hearing later."

The CHINS detention hearing. The words had a finality to them that Brock hadn't felt when Allison had first explained the intake process to him. He studied her now, wondering what she was thinking. She'd tried so hard to avoid this, to keep Joy from becoming part of the welfare system that she'd dedicated her life to and yet understood its failings. She would be so disappointed when the time came for the hearing. Already, he was disappointed enough for the both of them—and for Joy.

"Deputy Chandler, could you take the call on line two?" Jane called from the radio room.

Allison met his gaze, her own appearing hopeful. Did she still believe that the baby's mother would come through in the end and that her belief in people would be affirmed? Strange, he almost wished he could have a faith like that—in humanity and in God. He reached for the phone, hoping himself.

"What is it, Brock? Did she turn herself in?" Even as she asked the question, Allison already knew that wasn't it. She wanted to believe, and yet she was beginning not to be so sure. She didn't want to become as jaded as Brock, but she wondered if it was too late to prevent it.

Brock shook his head at her question, but already he was pushing back from his desk, his hands moving to the thick belt at his waist where he manually checked his gun and other equipment.

"It wasn't her. But we finally have a lead."

"What is it? Did the fingerprints bring up something?"

He frowned. "No, it's a hotel. It could be where the mother was staying. Somebody left a car seat in one of the rooms. One of the workers said he thinks he remembers a baby crying in that room."

"Why didn't they tell you that when you checked with all the hotels earlier?"

"This is a dive outside town. Clear Air. Or Clear Way or something. You know, the place with weekly rates instead of daily ones. I guess crying babies aren't so uncommon there."

"I know the place." Allison knew better than anyone that poorer areas didn't hold the market on child abuse, but she'd visited this motel for an investigation. "It's called the Clear View Motel, but it doesn't have a *clear view* of anything except the road out of town."

"Yeah, that's the one. Anyway, the maid went in to check the room— they only clean the rooms between guests. The girl had paid ahead and never checked out, so they didn't find the cast-off car seat until an hour ago."

Brock stepped over to a coatrack and pulled on his heavy sheriff's department jacket. "The manager said we were lucky the maid got sick of being with her family and came in to clean on Christmas Day." The side of his mouth pulled up when he turned back to her.

"If that family was getting along, we might not have gotten the clue until after New Year's Day," she said.

He studied her a few seconds, probably to see if she was joking, and then chuckled with her. "Either way, their discovery came too late. The mother could have skipped town right after the live nativity the other night."

"You're still going, right?"

"I'm still going."

Of course, he had to go. He had to do his job, just as she had to do hers, earlier that day and later at the hearing. But she didn't want him to leave any more than she wanted to get back in her own car and return to that depressing, empty house.

"Do you want me to help you out with those?" Brock didn't wait for an answer before stacking the packages in his arms.

"Thanks." She gathered a stack and turned back to him.

"It's going to take a second trip."

She nodded, wishing it could be a dozen instead of just two—anything to keep him with her a little longer. As it was, they had everything packed in her trunk and backseat far sooner than she would have liked.

"Well, I've got to get to the Clear View. I guess I'll see you—"

Allison shook her head to stop him. She knew what he was going to say—that he'd see her at the hearing. He didn't even have to be there, but she'd expected he would come. For Joy. Maybe even for her.

Still, she didn't even want to think about the hearing, let alone go to it. Worse than that, she didn't want to spend the next several hours at her house alone, waiting for the hearing she didn't want to attend. There had to be some way to stay busy and to stay away from the mausoleum she used to call home.

The idea that struck her then was like a gift from God—so simple, yet ingenious.

"Brock, you and I have both had jobs to do ever since Joy showed up in that manger."

"And your point is?" he asked when she didn't make one.

"My point is we both ultimately want the same thing for Joy—a safe home where she is loved."

Brock lifted an eyebrow, being generous by not pointing out that his goal also was to see the baby's mother behind bars.

"Well, the key to meeting our mutual goal is to find Joy's mother. Even if she wants to begin the Termination of Parental Rights process, we need to locate her."

He looked at her as if she was daft and spoke to her the way he would a child. "That's why I'm following up on this lead. To find the mother."

"I know you're doing your best, Brock. But I have an idea to make the search even better. Since we both need to find Joy's mom, I suggest that we combine our efforts."

"What are you saying?"

"I want us to team up, so we can find Joy's mother together."

Chapter Seven

Brock wondered if there were any other languages he could have said "Absolutely not" in and if any of them would have made a difference to Allison once she had her mind made up that he needed her help in this investigation. He guessed there were no others, at least none that would have changed her mind.

Even now as he stood in the abandoned hotel room with its threadbare sheets and scent of a recent insecticide spraying, he could still see her determination as clearly as when she'd announced her crazy idea of joining him. He'd fought a valiant fight at first, speaking of regulations and lawsuits and everything else he could pull from his debate arsenal. But then she'd turned her miserable expression on him, telling him she couldn't go back to that cold, empty house. He hadn't stood a chance.

"Joy and her mom probably stayed here."

Allison said the words without any judgment in her voice, but they condemned him anyway. She'd been right that first night when she'd reminded him they didn't know how desperate the mother's situation was. Pretty desperate, as far as he could tell.

"Not a four-star hotel, anyway."

"Not even one star," she concluded.

When Allison stepped to the bureau and started opening the drawers that swayed sideways from their broken tracks, Brock was glad he'd done at least one thing right tonight. He doubted, though, that having the forethought to make her wear latex gloves to eliminate her fingerprints would lessen his colossal mistake of letting her come.

"She didn't leave any clothes behind, for her or the baby," she said as she closed the second drawer.

"She probably didn't have much."

His comment must have surprised her as much as it had him because she turned and met his gaze too long, until he looked away. What had she thought before, that he didn't have a heart? She just didn't understand. He didn't have the luxury of pitying the suspect in his investigation, of wondering if the woman might have deserted her child to protect her from living this life.

Remember that I love you. The mother's words on that note troubled him just as they had when they'd first found it. If that mother had wanted better for her child, could it mean that just possibly, his own mother had left for *his* benefit? No, he would never believe that. Madeline didn't have an unselfish bone in her body. He'd been a burden she'd unloaded without ever looking back.

For several seconds he stared at the outdated and stained car seat in the corner where a casualty of extermination efforts also lay, its six legs up in the air. Joy's mother might have been trying to do that right thing, but the way she'd gone about it was a crime. His job was to enforce the laws, not to weigh in with his opinion on whether or not they were properly merciful. No matter how much they wished it otherwise, few people were ever on the receiving end of mercy.

Allison, who had slipped into the tiny bathroom a few minutes before, popped her head out. "Brock, do you know if the maid actually cleaned the room or just opened it up to clean it and found the car seat?"

He lifted his own gloved hand from where he was tracing a finger though a trail of dust likely far older than Joy. "The manager said she started to clean but stopped when she found the car seat. Why do you ask?"

"Come look at this."

The mildew-filled scent caught him as he stepped to the bathroom doorway. Black lines of it covered the grout on sections of crumbling tile.

She pointed to the trash basket. "Most people leave some sort of waste behind—tissues, cotton balls, something. She had a baby in this room, and yet there aren't any soiled diapers."

"So she might have emptied her own trash. Or the maid might have done it."

"Either way, we don't have a lot to go on. You can learn a lot about a person by the things she throws away."

Brock couldn't help grinning. "Been watching a lot of crime investigation shows lately?"

She shrugged and smiled back. "They're interesting."

"We don't even know how long she's been gone."

Even he could hear the frustration in his voice. "The desk clerk couldn't remember for sure which day he'd heard the crying. And if the guest was our suspect, she might have cruised out of here right after she dropped off the baby. If so, she'd be long gone by now."

"Or maybe not," she said softly, but her wary expression showed she wasn't holding out much hope.

Because the room suddenly felt too quiet, too close, both returned to their individual observations. He had to give Joy's mom credit. She'd been neat, and she hadn't left anything behind that wouldn't require a specially trained crime scene investigator to find it.

For a long time, Brock and Allison worked companionably in the small space, neither breaking the silence with unnecessary words. Whether it was a mistake or not to have done it, he was glad he'd brought her along to keep him company today. It *was* Christmas, after all. He didn't want to be alone, either, as he searched for clues.

Not that they were really accomplishing anything by being here or could even know for sure that Joy had been in that car seat, though his gut told him that the baby from this room and the child in the manger were onc in the same. Did Allison realize like he did that they were no closer to locating Baby Doe's mother than they were the moment they realized something was fishy about those swaddling clothes?

"You haven't failed her, you know." He wished he could have stopped them, but the words seemed just to fall from his lips of their own accord.

Allison jerked her head and turned back to him, her eyes too shiny. "I just thought—"

"That she would come back?" Another day he might have said, "I told you so." Any woman who'd managed to vanish like that wouldn't reappear and call it all a big misunderstanding. He'd known that truth, but still Allison had kept hoping. Brock hated knowing that she wouldn't believe anymore. He wished he could make it right for her, restore her faith.

And suddenly he was saying ridiculous things for no other reason than that he had to try. For her sake. "We still have a few hours until the hearing. I doubt we're going to find anything else here. Let's go back to the department and look over the case file again. Maybe there's something we've missed."

Because she was nodding enthusiastically, he kept on going, each word feeling like more of a lie than the last. But this was worse than just fooling her with words she wanted to believe. He was fooling himself, as well. He wanted to believe it, too.

"We'll check with the hospitals again. Maybe they've found a patient's record that they overlooked before. We'll check with state police for anyone picked up for hitchhiking from the area."

Allison rushed over to the door, speaking over her shoulder as she went. "Somebody must have seen her. We just haven't asked the right people yet."

No, they hadn't asked the right people. But he and the other deputies had canvassed the town, asking everyone they could think of—gas station attendants, truck drivers, convenience store clerks—if they'd seen anyone out of the ordinary. Someone who might meet the general description of the woman witnesses saw the night of the live nativity.

The quiet descended again as Allison waited at the door and Brock took one last look around the hotel room.

"Brock, tell me about when your parents deserted you."

His sharp intake of breath stung his lungs, but he forced himself to at least appear relaxed. "They didn't desert me. Roy and Clara Chandler, both of them, were with me every minute I'd let them, until the days they died."

"You know what I mean. Tell me about Madeline and…I don't think you said his name."

Brock's heart squeezed, and not just because Allison had remembered his birth mother's name. He'd carried all of this pain inside an awfully long time. It was heavy. He didn't want to carry it anymore.

"I don't even *know* his name, but Madeline Jeffries, I won't forget that. She liked me to call her Madeline in public. Not Mom. Not Mommy. Those words put a dent in her social life."

"I'm so sorry—"

But he waved a hand to interrupt her. He'd started telling this in the same way a freight train started moving—slowly, reluctantly. Now there didn't seem to be anything he could do to stop it all from rolling forward, even if he was acting both the role of tiny boy balancing on the railroad tracks and the engineer trying desperately to avoid a catastrophe.

"We used to play this game where I pretended in front of her *friends* that I was her neighbor's kid, and she was only watching me. If I pretended well and went right to bed, I'd get candy in the morning."

"But you loved her."

Because she didn't say it as a question, he didn't bother trying to deny it. "When it was just the two of us at home, she'd let me curl her long hair around my fingers. She even let me call her Mommy then."

"So what happened?"

"One day, she dropped me off at the day-care center, kissed me goodbye and never came back."

Though he hadn't been watching her until then, Brock looked up, expecting to see pity in her eyes. Instead, she approached him slowly and took his hand in hers. Her eyes glistened with tears, and a few spilled over.

Brock had to force himself to remain still when his instinct was to gather her into his arms, comforting her and, for once, allowing another human to console him. He tried to chuckle as he gently pulled his hand away, but it came out sounding strange to his ears.

"Come on, it's not a sad story. I couldn't have had better parents than Roy and Clara. He coached soccer. She taught my Sunday school class."

Instead of commenting on his quick segue from his scars, she smiled. "I'm so glad they were there for you."

"They taught me about God's love and lived their entire lives being living examples of it."

Allison opened her mouth, and then she snapped it shut. He could guess what she was about to ask.

"Oh, sorry about my comments the other night. The ones about God. As you can tell, the whole abandonment issue hits close to home."

"I understand."

Brock sensed that she did understand, more than just the excuse for his verbal attacks. As he followed her to the door and reached around her to open it, he hoped she would also understand that he couldn't dwell on his past now, not if they were going to find the missing clue that would lead them to Joy's mother.

The suspect, though, had disappeared into thin air. They were attempting to pluck her back out of that air. The clock was ticking until the detention hearing. For Allison—and especially for Joy—he had to try.

In the light of day, the stable just looked like a rustic lean-to with a bunch of hay bales and a wooden trough in it. But as Allison drew in a lungful of the crisp air that announced Indiana's white Christmas would be arriving a day or so too late, she could envision it all. David fidgeting with his Joseph hat. Her pillow belly falling out. The choir guys in their Wise Men's robes.

Because she wanted to keep her gaze from returning again and again to the manger bed, she concentrated on the hay scent that wafted in her nostrils. The memory of the pony's neigh, so out of place and yet not, tickled her ears. She heard the choir…heard the cry.

And Brock was there, appearing like a bright light out of the darkened crowd.

He'd done the same thing in her life, coming so quickly into focus while the rest of her life before him remained a blur. As terrifying as not knowing was, she didn't want the blur back for anything in the world.

"Why do you think she did it?"

She jerked her head to look at Brock as he again scanned the area where they'd found the diaper bag and the Baby Jesus doll, as if the scene would somehow speak to him and provide the answers that had eluded them.

"You mean why she abandoned the baby?"

"Yeah, in your professional opinion."

She slowly shook her head. "I don't know. There can be all kinds of extenuating circumstances, plenty of stress factors. If she would only come forward, we could look at all of the stressors affecting her."

"Some examples?"

"She might have four other kids at home and can't afford to feed another. This child might have been the product of an adulterous affair, and she couldn't bring her home. There might be physical abuse in the home. She could be a drug addict or a teen mom or be mentally ill." Allison crossed to the manger, her hand automatically brushing the hay in it. "Enough?"

"So it could have been almost anything?"

She nodded as she approached the hay bale where he stood. "It doesn't mean she doesn't love her child. And, Brock—" she paused until he met her gaze "—just because your mom left doesn't mean she didn't love you, either."

"But not enough, right?"

"Maybe more than you know. Maybe she wanted to give you the chance for a better life."

* * *

Allison unlocked the front door, her hand that held the key feeling as heavy as her heart. No, nothing could compare to her heart.

"You sure you're going to be okay?" Brock asked.

"Yeah, I'm just tired." She stepped inside the door, slipped off her coat and hung it on the coat tree.

She wondered why she bothered lying when the man standing behind her in her entry so obviously didn't believe her. He'd asked how she was three times since he'd led her to his car, suggesting that she leave hers downtown and pick it up in the morning.

She wasn't all right. How could she be? The hearing had come and gone. She'd submitted the 311 investigative report with more than enough factors to substantiate child neglect: abandonment, lack of supervision and lack of food, shelter and clothing.

And Joy had officially become a Child in Need of Services.

An unrelenting fist seized Allison's heart, squeezing. She'd failed Joy. No amount of investigating had put them any closer to finding the baby's mother and avoiding Joy's big welcome into the system.

This wasn't the first time she'd ever felt as if she'd failed one of the children in her case files; it was an unfortunate drawback of the job. The pain this time felt more acute, though, physical proof that she'd become too attached. She needed to distance herself, from the baby and probably from the deputy who had as much invested in the case as she did.

A warm hand came to rest on her shoulder then, and she knew she didn't want him to leave.

"You did all you could for her."

"I know, but—"

"But nothing. She's lucky to have you on her side."

"I just wish—"

He interrupted her by squeezing her shoulder as if to say that he understood, and like her, he wished. "I know."

Heat and comfort seemed to flow from his fingertips through her sweater and into her skin. It was the first time she'd been warm all day. The connection was all too brief as he pulled his hand away. A void remained where his touch had lingered.

Brock cleared his throat. "I don't know about you, but I'm starved. Did we eat anything today?"

"Only things from the vending machine that should have had labels saying, 'Danger! Artery Clogging.'"

"Didn't you say you had several Christmas dinner invitations? You should have gone instead of hanging out at the sheriff's department. You could have been eating plum pudding instead of mini doughnuts."

She smiled. "Nah, plum pudding's overrated."

"But I'd still eat some if we could find any right now." He indicated her kitchen with a jerk of his head. "You…um…got anything to eat?"

She laughed out loud at that. It felt good to laugh, almost as good as it felt to be near Brock, even if he was probably only sticking around to cheer her up. He probably was disappointed in himself for failing to save the day.

"That's a unique way to finagle a dinner invitation. I'll have to try it someday."

"You might want to reserve judgment until I find out how successful my ploy is."

She shook her head and grinned. "Brock, would you like to stay for Christmas dinner?"

Chapter Eight

At Allison's invitation, Brock relaxed for the first time since they'd left the courthouse. She'd been so quiet, so obviously distressed, that he'd worried she would insist on being alone when he'd wanted to be there for her. Just as much, he wanted to be there for himself.

"Okay, you can use my method for getting invited to dinner. It works pretty well, if I do say so myself." He wiggled his eyebrow.

"Next time you'll probably want to make sure your potential host has a fully stocked pantry before you get yourself invited. I don't even know what I've got."

Before she became self-conscious about her empty cupboards and reneged on her invitation, he motioned for her to follow and led her into the kitchen. "We'll just have to get creative then."

He was pleased with himself a half hour later when they were seated cross-legged on the floor beside the coffee table, a potluck spread of canned ravioli, carrot sticks and peanut butter toast on the table before them.

Several ceramic figurines had to be moved to the floor to make room for the food.

"Everything tastes wonderful," she said, before taking another big bite of the gooey, melted peanut butter.

"If you like this, you should really let me cook for you sometime."

Her startled expression showed that what he'd said had surprised her, too. The words had escaped before he could stop them, but he couldn't deny the truth in them. No matter how bad an idea it was, he wanted to see her again.

Maybe the need to reach out to Allison only struck him now because the hearing was over, and they no longer had the excuse of Joy's case to keep them in contact. He could also blame his frustration over failing in his first worthwhile Cox County investigation—failing Joy. The reason didn't matter. The fact remained.

For several seconds, Allison studied her food, swirling the ravioli in its artificially red sauce. "You don't strike me as the cooking type."

He wanted to kiss her for giving him a break by glossing over the fact that he'd just asked her out. The thought made him smile as he studied the lips she patted nervously with her napkin. He wanted to kiss her, all right, but for many reasons. Her innate charity was just one of them.

"What would I have to do to look like the cooking type—wear a chef's hat and wave around a wooden spoon?"

"No, but I'd like to see that."

Allison's laugh was as close to a girlish giggle as

he'd heard from her, and he was pleased with himself at having inspired it. Her face appeared so soft. Relaxed. Young. Had she ever been the carefree girl he glimpsed now, or had life always gotten in the way of her happiness?

The injustice of it struck him suddenly, deeply, in a place he'd thought reserved only for his own pain. She deserved happiness—complete, delirious happiness—where she didn't have to carry the weight of everyone else's problems on her shoulders. Strange how he wished he could be the man to help her to find it, but how could he help her discover something he'd never known himself?

"Do you ever think that sometimes we're put in situations for a purpose, even when we don't understand what it is?"

Brock swallowed and tried not to wonder if she'd been reading his mind. "You mean does God put us there?" He waited for her nod before he added, "I don't know."

"Don't you think He intended our lives to cross with Joy's?" She didn't mention two other lives that had crossed, but it was understood.

"Does that also mean God planned for the baby's mother to leave her in the stable?" He watched as her relaxed posture tightened, and he shook his head. "Even I don't believe that. Not really."

Her smile returned like buds on a white oak after a freezing Indiana winter. He held his breath not to sigh with relief.

"I knew you didn't."

"You think you know a lot about me, don't you?"

"Only what you tell me."

He smiled at that, not believing it for a minute. "But you have theories, right?"

She traced her finger through the peanut butter on her last piece of toast, her gaze focused on the swirls, before she looked up at him again. "I think it's hard for you to trust. People. Anything."

He would have wondered just when he had lost the upper hand in the conversation, but for a reason he couldn't explain, he'd handed it over to her like a gift.

"Anything else?"

"Isn't that enough?"

"I guess. But I trusted my parents—Roy and Clara. Implicitly. So how does that fit in with your theory?" And he trusted Allison. He didn't know how to process that realization, but he did trust her.

"I don't know. Maybe I'm wrong about you."

He shook his head. "Not wrong."

"What about God? Do you trust Him?"

With a carrot stick, he stirred the remaining tomato sauce on his plate. How could he answer that? Would she turn her back on him when he did?

"I have faith," he said finally. "That has to be enough. I don't think God wants us to lie around and wait for Him to take care of us, anyway."

Her smile was warm, as though she remembered something precious. "God has always been my lifeline. When Mom was sick, I don't know what I would have done without Him. Like that poem about the footprints in the sand, He carried me through the darkest days."

"The way you carried your mother." He didn't ask it as a question because he already knew the answer. She'd carried too much for far too long.

"I guess so. But what was I to do? She needed me."

"What about your sister?"

"She was married. She had a life."

"You had a life, too, didn't you?"

She shrugged. "It was easier for me. I was able to get a job at the Division of Family and Children, take night classes to finish my master's in social work and still be here for Mom. It was the best solution."

"For everyone else or for you?" He glanced around the living room that he'd come to resent because it represented all that had been taken from her. "Even now, you're still living in her house and not getting on with your life."

Coming up off the floor, Allison planted her hands on her hips. "I am getting on with—"

"You don't travel. You're not married. You don't date, not even that guy, David, who played Joseph."

She stopped and stared at him, her cheeks flushed. "How do you know all that?"

"Are you kidding? You've lived your whole life in a small town, and you don't know how news gets around?"

"Oh. Right." Quiet for several seconds, she crouched and started stacking the dishes. "Well, according to the ladies at the county assessor's office, you didn't arrive in town with a wife and a passel of kids. If their sources are accurate, there's no fiancée or girlfriend, either."

"Good sources. There's never been a fiancée, and the

girlfriend's been out of the picture since a corporate at-torney gave her a better offer." That Robin had started dating said attorney behind his back had a lot to do with why he didn't trust women. At least it was part of it. He didn't tell Allison that. He was much more interested in finding out about her, anyway. "What about you? Is your dating record any better?"

Instead of laughing, the way he'd hoped, she stared at the ground. "Not everyone gets what she wants in life."

"What do *you* want, Allison? Do you want to spend the rest of your life surrounded by stuff that isn't yours, living a life that isn't yours, one that's more inherited than chosen?"

At first she wouldn't meet his gaze, but when she did, the hurt in her eyes sliced him like a freshly sharpened knife, its cut clean but going clear to the bone. He had no excuse for being so harsh. How could her promise for a future matter more to him than it did to her? But it did. It was as if his life depended on it, too.

"Didn't you ever have dreams?" Even he could hear the emotion in his voice.

When she lifted her gaze to meet his again, her eyes shone. "I had dreams like any other girl. But that's just it. Dreams are for children. You know, it's like that passage in I Corinthians Chapter 13 that says, 'When I was a child, I spake as a child, I understood as a child: but when I became a man…'" She paused. "A woman."

Instead of waiting, Brock finished for her. "'I put away childish things.' Are you serious? Do you really believe that God would ask you to put away your dreams?"

"If His plans for me were different…then maybe."

"What did you dream about?"

Allison looked away from him, fussing again with the remaining dishes and placing the figurines back in their places. "Just the usual things—a home, kids, a husband." She shrugged. "One out of three isn't bad."

She probably hoped he would laugh at her feeble attempt at humor, but he wasn't biting. Instead, he stayed quiet and waited.

Finally, she turned back to him the way he'd hoped she would. Her gaze met his. Held.

And he knew. Well, he wondered, anyway, because he wasn't certain of anything lately, least of all his former commitment to keeping his distance from people. Did she see him as someone she could love? And if she did, would he ever have the guts to risk loving her back?

Instead of carrying the dishes to the kitchen, Allison set them on the floor and crossed to the picture window. For several minutes, she stared out into the darkness of the waning hours of Christmas Day, twinkling holiday lights outlining the other homes of Destiny and the day's first snowflakes dancing to the ground. Brock rose from the floor and approached her from behind, holding his hands at his sides to keep from touching her.

Without looking back at him, she spoke again. "With me, it really isn't about giving up childish things and the dream of finding someone. It's about losing hope."

Hope? How could she believe that she'd never find someone to love, someone who would love her? He wondered what she imagined when she looked in the mirror, because she obviously didn't see a beautiful, vibrant woman in the glass. The woman he saw.

Before him she stood, her shoulders hung forward as if the weight of her life had become too heavy. Someone needed to help her carry her load this time. Was he strong enough to be that someone?

His hands curled over her shoulders before he had the chance to think the situation through and to convince himself to be sensible. Beneath his fingertips, he could feel her tremble. At least he thought it was her, though his insides shook with the fear of doing the wrong thing, the anxiety of missing the chance to do the right one.

"Never give up hope, Allison," he whispered, not certain she even heard him.

Strange, he'd expected her to shy away from his touch, but she straightened her shoulders beneath his hands, as if his presence made her feel stronger. He could relate. A missing puzzle piece in his heart snapped into place as he continued to hold her, both of them staring out at the last lights of Christmas. He could have stood there forever as the moment became his measuring stick for perfection.

But Allison moved her right arm across to her left shoulder and covered his hand with hers. Slowly, he turned her to face him and drew her into the circle of his arms. There, before the picture window and thousands of twinkling lights, he tasted the wonder of her kiss. The moment was precious and startling because he could imagine himself repeating it hundreds of times, each time feeling new like the first.

But as he opened his eyes and pulled away, the shock

on her face sent him sprinting back to reality. He let his hands fall to his sides. Kissing her had been a mistake. And yet, how could a mistake have felt so right— a pristine, unbroken vow shining in contrast to the sea of forsaken promises all around it?

Allison was still staring at him, wide-eyed, and chewing on her lower lip. "I'd better…" Instead, of finishing, she stepped past him and collected the stack of dishes on the floor.

"Let me help." He grabbed the second stack and followed her into the kitchen.

Neither spoke as they stood in the narrow area by the sink, loading the dishwasher. A third entity—the kiss—cramped the space even more by squeezing between them. By the time Allison started the wash cycle, it was clear their fairy-tale Christmas night was over.

He dried his hands on a kitchen towel. "Thanks for having me, but I'd better get home. Everyone else might be returning pea-green sweaters and solar-powered bun warmers tomorrow, but for the sheriff's department, it will be back to business as usual." He grinned. "Oh, I guess it will be different. Just one shift instead of holiday overtime."

"I have to work, too." Allison smiled back, but she still wrung her hands together.

Awkwardness had seeped into their budding friendship and refused to leave. He tried to hide his disappointment as he made his less-than-debonair escape, berating himself about the kiss all the way to his apartment.

It had to have been hormones rather than any actual

brain activity that had driven his thinking for him to do something so stupid, so rash. He couldn't explain why he'd had to go and ruin the best night he could remember in a long time—maybe ever—by crossing the line between friendship and a deeper relationship.

He should have known she wasn't ready. Ready? Whatever had happened to *him* not being ready for female companionship and to his certainty if he made himself vulnerable to any woman, he'd only be risking heartbreak? At least his mother and Robin had taught him one life skill. Too bad when he was around Allison, he didn't have the sense to come in out of the rain—or at least to stay away from her house.

Rather than kissing her, he should have just taken out a billboard advertisement to announce that in the few days since Allison had shown up in his life dressed in her biblical finest, he'd lost all his good sense. Why couldn't he just have kept his distance from her, where he could have protected his heart?

But a strange thought struck him. For the first time, he didn't want to live safely. He'd been certain of little lately, yet he was convinced that he wanted to be with Allison. For her sake as much as his. She needed someone to show her that she was worthy of love—that he just might already love her. Shaking his head in the darkness, he mounted the steps to his apartment, one of four efficiencies in a converted house on Elm.

People didn't fall in love after only a few days. It was almost as bad as love at first sight though he'd had an extra forty-eight hours to convince himself what he'd seen and felt wasn't real. And he'd failed. He still wanted to be near her, to hear her clever theories on his case, even to be comforted in knowing that people like her still existed—those who found the good in others and believed in God's promises without being like Thomas and having to touch Christ's scars. For the first time, he wanted to be like that, to walk the tightrope of his life without a safety net. To finally put his trust in someone.

Are you sorry you kissed her? he asked himself as he unlocked the door and pushed inside. The immediate tingling around his mouth gave his answer away. Not only was he *not* sorry, except for maybe his timing, he was perfectly willing to kiss her again anytime she asked. And he hoped with all his heart she would ask.

Too tired to think any longer, Brock slumped out of his clothes and climbed beneath the sheets. In that place between slumber and alertness, her image drifted through his thoughts. She was smiling at him this time, not nervous as she'd been earlier. He gave himself up to sleep and to the notion that when it came to Allison Hensley, he was lost.

Chapter Nine

Allison flipped on the lights at the Division of Family and Children, wishing the thermos of coffee she'd already consumed would finally kick in. She must have tried closing her eyes a hundred times last night with the purpose of shutting out her thoughts and her confusion, but both had followed her, sleep the casualty of their pursuit.

From the moment that Brock had closed the door to separate them, she'd felt lonelier than at any time since her mother had died. The house, so full of things, seemed empty now. How, in just a few days, could she have gone from feeling contented in her single life to so dissatisfied?

Shaking her head, she sat at her desk and booted up her PC. She hadn't been content before, not really. *Resigned* was a better word for it, a word that brought no glory to God if He really did want her to lead a single life. As if her lot in life was so horrible that she could find no joy in living it.

Admitting she'd been dissatisfied long before Brock

had sauntered in and thrown her world off its axis felt like a betrayal to her mother's memory and to God's plans for her life.

What if you were wrong? The question plagued her as it had all night while she'd tossed and turned and tried to hide from feelings she couldn't define. What if God had a different plan for her life other than the one she had formed in her own disappointment and convinced herself to accept? What if He'd never intended for her to be alone and had planned to answer her questions in His time? What if she hadn't been listening?

But even if God did have someone in mind for her, she couldn't imagine Brock being His choice. Brock, the man who clearly had difficulty trusting women and would never trust her with his heart. She would never be able to live with someone's love but not his trust.

She thought back to that night at the live nativity. Not once had Brock considered that Joy's mother would return for her the way Allison had hoped she would. That he'd been right didn't make the fact any less telling. Brock probably wasn't the man for her.

So why did her heart cry out for him? She'd been held before, been kissed before, so why did her mind refuse to stop replaying his embrace?

Tears of frustration clouded her vision as she stared at the computer screen, still seeing only the moment when she'd been in the circle of Brock's arms and feeling whole in a way she'd never known before.

"Hey, you're in early," Clara Johnson called as she dumped her purse and briefcase in her office and then came out to face Allison's desk while still wearing her coat. "I thought you'd schlep in after nine, calling for fairness and comp time or some other nonsense."

"I hope you had a good Christmas, too."

"All the toys are broken, the CD's are scratched and none of the clothes fit, but it was all mistletoe and holly for us. Are you still full of the Yuletide spirit?"

Allison gave her boss a sad smile, wishing Clara, too, could know the true meaning of Christmas. "I did take that little donkey ride to Bethlehem."

"And took one humongous detour, didn't you?" Clara laughed. "All in a day's work for a family case manager."

She tried to laugh with her. It had been a detour, all right. From her play. From her life. And she wasn't at all sure how to get back on the right path—the one leading home.

Instead of hanging up her coat, Clara picked up a file from her desk and grabbed her briefcase again. "Can you believe they scheduled a meeting at the courthouse this early on the day after Christmas? That's just not right." She crossed to the office door and turned back to Allison. "You'll hold down the fort, right?"

Again, she nodded, wondering what she would do with herself in the silence until the agency's only other FCM arrived that afternoon. She heard the scrape of the heavy glass office door as her boss headed out into the snow that was finally accumulating.

Turning back to the computer, she pulled up a file on five-year-old twin boys whose parents would be in court later in the week. The boys would forever bear the scars of the accidental fire they'd caused while their parents were out partying, but Allison resigned herself to the reality that those boys would be going back home. She could only hope that the court-required drug counseling and parenting classes had taught the parents something about caring for their kids.

A scrape of the metal-and-glass door on its frame brought her attention up from the computer screen. "Did you forget something?" she called out to her boss. "You're going to be late, and you know how Judge Douglas hates that."

She expected a hearty laugh and a nasty comment from the person entering the office, but she only heard approaching footsteps on the squeaky floor. An uncomfortable sensation settled between her shoulder blades as she came up from her desk and started toward the outer office. Anyone showing up this early the day after Christmas when the rest of the community was still recovering wouldn't have a pretty story to tell.

A female visitor, her hair and part of her face obscured beneath the hood of a heavy wool coat, hesitated just outside the open office area Allison shared with the other family case manager. Allison's breath caught in her throat. Hadn't the witnesses from the other night mentioned a long, hooded coat? Could it be her?

She would have berated herself again for refusing to surrender her rose-colored glasses in wishing for Joy's mother's return if the woman didn't lower her hood to reveal a swollen, tearstained face. She wasn't a woman at all, but a girl of maybe fifteen or sixteen, who from the look of her had known more pain than years.

"I'm looking for Allison Hensley," the girl said with

an unsteady voice. She remained just outside the office, fidgeting and shooting glances toward the exit.

"I'm Allison." She took a step closer but stopped as the girl stiffened even more. Instinct told her she might bolt, so Allison remained as still as she could, waiting for the girl to say something.

"I saw your name in the newspaper article about the baby in the manger." She chewed her lower lip. "You were Mary in the live nativity scene."

"Yes, I was." Allison smiled, hoping to encourage the girl to relax. "You seem to know who I am, but I don't know who you are."

The girl stared at her hands. "I'm Tracie Long."

Allison waited, trying not to pad the uncomfortable silence with idle chatter. Tracie stood without speaking, her stricken face a mirror for the battle that appeared to wage inside her. Finally, a pair of tears escaped her fierce hold and trailed down her cheeks.

Forgetting her caution, Allison moved forward until they were face-to-face, though the girl looked at the ground instead of her. "Tracie, let me help."

Finally, she lifted her head and met Allison's gaze. "I'm the baby's mother."

Brock's gaze was distant, hard, as he greeted Allison and Tracie at the front door of the sheriff's department not twenty minutes later. Obviously, he didn't have an ounce of compassion to spare for the petite teenager who cowered the minute she saw him.

"Miss Long, come this way please." He led them to

an interview room with a long metal table and folding chairs as the only accoutrements.

Instead of offering the sixteen-year-old anything to drink, the deputy only sat across from her and flipped open a spiral-topped notebook. He was being so impossibly insensitive that Allison wondered why he didn't just snap the handcuffs on Tracie right then. At least he couldn't force Allison to leave the room, since Tracie's parents had stipulated during their telephone conversation that she be there for the interview.

"It's okay, Tracie. Go ahead and tell us what happened," Allison encouraged. "Your parents are on their way from Ohio, and they'll be here in a few hours."

But the minute the teen opened her mouth to speak, the tears began again. "I need to know…is she okay? Is she eating enough? Does she still have her nights and days mixed up?"

Brock cleared his throat. "You lost the right to ask questions when you dumped your baby in a feeding trough."

Tracie's head shot back, as if she'd been slapped, and her tears came harder.

Allison wanted to throw her body across the table to shield the teenager from Brock's censuring glare. They didn't even know yet what Tracie had to say.

"Your baby's fine, Tracie," Allison said. "The family that's caring for her loves children."

The gratitude that danced in Tracie's eyes, along with her tears, was nearly Allison's undoing.

"I thought…I could…do it," the girl began. "I thought

we'd all be okay once I brought Christina Marie home from the hospital."

Christina Marie Long? Allison rolled the name around on her tongue, but it just didn't sound right. The baby was Joy, would always be Joy in her heart.

When Tracie's voice broke, and she sobbed into her hands, Brock simply glanced up from his notebook, reached for a box of tissues and handed them to her.

"Go ahead, Miss Long."

Tracie made several ineffectual swipes at her face and tried again. "But my parents—they were embarrassed by me. By us."

"And the baby's father?" Allison couldn't help asking. Her question only earned her a scowl from Brock.

The teenager shrugged. "He doesn't want anything to do with her or me."

"Did you think if you deserted the child, he would take you back?"

Had the audible gasp been Tracie's or her own? Allison couldn't tell which. Tracie appeared shocked by Brock's question. Brock's expression only showed disdain.

Tracie started shaking her head. "No…no…no. It's not like that." A sob escaped her again. "Not like that at all."

Allison reached over and squeezed her arm. "Then tell us what it was like."

She didn't care what Brock thought about her interrupting his questioning again. How dare he be so stoic when the girl's heart was breaking and likely had been broken again and again by all that had taken place?

Tracie spoke of her naive plans to run away and build a life for herself and baby Christina. Of ending up at the Clear View Motel and realizing how little she had to offer her child.

"When I saw a flyer about the live nativity scene, it suddenly seemed to be the answer to my prayers. I knew she would be found. I knew she would be safe."

The sides of Tracie's mouth turned up in a small smile, the first Allison had seen since the girl walked into her office.

"Were you aware it's a crime to abandon a child?" Brock asked.

Tracie shook her head at first and then said, "I don't know what I thought. I love my baby. I wanted to give her the life she deserves."

"You must think she deserves a life in foster care because that's what you've given her."

"Brock!" His name came out as a single sharp syllable, but Allison couldn't stop herself. Was this the man she loved, a man who could be so cruel? Her own heart ached for Tracie, who had been faced with nothing but difficult choices. The girl had made the wrong decision, but she'd done it out of love. Could she say the same for Brock's behavior?

Allison cleared her throat and spoke to the girl instead of him.

"Deputy Chandler is trying to say that no matter whether you were trying to do the right thing for your child or not, you still broke the law. You might face criminal charges for abandoning your baby."

She waited for Tracie's nod of understanding before

she continued. "Even if you don't face charges, you'll want to consider the option of signing a voluntary termination of parental rights so that your baby can be adopted."

Allison cringed inside when thinking of the formal court hearing that such a termination would require— an event so final that many had described it as a death. She couldn't imagine ever willingly letting go of Joy.

Brock pushed back from the table and paced, his movements short, annoyed.

For several seconds, Tracie watched him but then turned back to Allison. Her shoulders straightening, the girl appeared far older than her sixteen years. "I'm ready to face the consequences for what I did."

"It's up to the court now," Allison said.

Tracie nodded and lowered her gaze to study her folded hands. When she spoke again, her voice was soft. "God had special plans for that first child found in a manger. I'd hoped the Father might have plans for my baby, too."

The girl's words hounded him as Brock typed up the report. *God had special plans...* No, he didn't want to think about that, didn't want to allow himself to lose his focus.

He glanced over to the interview room where Tracie Long was inside, having a conference with Allison and her parents. Allison had explained that she needed to talk with the girl and her parents to find out what the stressors were for the family and what were the safety risks for Tracie and for her child in that household. As if any *stressor* would justify what she'd done.

Allison hadn't said a word to him since they'd first interviewed Tracie together. Clearly, she thought he'd been too tough on the girl. He was just doing his job, just as he had been all along since that first night in the stable. Allison needed to understand that.

Well, his first major investigation was solved, whether he'd been the one to find the suspect or not. He tried not to be annoyed that the girl had turned herself in to the Division of Family and Children rather than the sheriff's department. A woman who portrayed Jesus' mother probably seemed more approachable than people with badges, anyway, especially to a teenager.

Funny, he'd expected to feel satisfaction when he took Joy's mother into custody. Instead, he felt only relief. Tracie was little more than a child herself, and she'd had a child of her own. Hardly the evil woman he'd been hunting when he'd begun the investigation.

But the girl had abandoned her child, he reminded himself. The baby, Joy, was the victim. He shook his head to dispel the artificial name from it. Christina Marie Long was her name, and she'd been deserted just as he had. He closed his eyes, trying not to become that little lost boy again, but the emptiness overwhelmed him against his will. No one had been around to defend him, but he was there for this baby, no matter what her name was.

As for the mother, she'd broken the law. She'd even confessed to the crime, which could end up in the juvenile or adult courts, depending on the county prosecutor's decision. Whether or not the girl would go to prison for her crime, he could only guess. The courts would look at things such as motive and extenuating circumstances, so he shouldn't waste his time doing it.

His job was to enforce the law. It was as black and white as that. But for the first time, child abandonment seemed to have its share of grays. Tracie—he wanted to think of her as "the suspect," but he just couldn't—had left her child, not because she didn't love her, but because she did. The realization tempted him to wonder about another mother and another set of circumstances.

Strange, he'd never thought about it that way before, but it didn't matter why his mother had done it because her decision—selfless or selfish—had landed him just where he was supposed to be, with the Chandlers. His real family. His birth mother's decision had made it possible for him to grow up in a home built with more than bricks and mortar but constructed of love for family and for God. Could anyone ask for more than that? So why had he spent his lifetime wishing for more?

Chapter Ten

Wet snowflakes landed on her eyelashes just after seven o'clock that night as Allison waved goodbye to the Longs in the sheriff's department parking lot. At least Tracie had been released into her parents' custody until her initial court appearance the next morning.

Tracie looked so small as she waved from the car's back window. It would be a long night for the Long family as they went to their hotel and continued the discussion they'd started in the interview room a few hours before.

How did a family get so far off track? she wondered. When had it become more important what others at church thought about their parenting of Tracie than their actual job of raising their daughter? Could any mistake a child made be bad enough for a parent to stop loving her? That wasn't fair, and she knew it. Tracie's parents did love her, or they wouldn't have come all the way to central Indiana to be with her.

Sure, this whole mess had begun with Tracie's mistake of trying to use sex to keep a boyfriend who wasn't worth keeping, but her parents had contributed to this sad outcome. They hadn't thrown her out, but they'd let their shame prevent them from helping her make the best of a difficult situation. They'd refused to forgive, and it had only multiplied their pain.

They were so much like Brock who wouldn't, or maybe couldn't, let go of his anger toward his mother. His anger had prevented him from opening his heart to love. She'd known that before and had convinced herself she could reach past his walls. Only today had she understood how hard his pent-up fury had made him.

Tracie hoped God had plans for her child in the manger. Had Allison been just kidding herself when she'd imagined the Father's plans for her and Brock? It couldn't have been more clear to her now that she'd been wrong to wish it. She couldn't see God ever choosing a future for her with a man who had no compassion in his heart, couldn't even muster a little for a hurting sixteen-year-old girl.

Hopelessness covered Allison as realization settled heavily in her heart. But the truth was immovable. She couldn't allow herself to love a man who had no compassion, no matter how much it hurt to let go of her dreams.

Staring across the nearly empty street, she reached up to touch her hair, damp from the fluttering snow-flakes. A chill crawled up her arms, making her shiver as she approached her car, dreading having to scrape her windows.

"Allison, wait up."

His voice drifted up behind her like a wave at high

tide, washing over her and then drawing her out to sea and back to him. She couldn't let him pull her back. She needed to protect her heart by walking away from him.

"It's been a long day. I need to get home," she said without stopping or turning around.

His stride was longer than hers, so he easily caught up with her and rested a hand on her shoulder. At his touch, warmth seeped through her heavy coat and beneath her skin. It was too late to protect her tender emotions when he'd already sneaked in and taken possession of her heart.

"You're angry." He squeezed her shoulder again and released it. "I had a job to do, just like you do."

Brock studied her as she turned to face him, her eyebrow raised.

"I know that."

"Do you?"

That she just stood there and said nothing answered the question. She didn't understand him any better than he'd been able to understand Tracie's motivation for leaving her child as a set prop.

Nervous energy had him rubbing his freezing hands together. "Being tough on the girl was just part of questioning. We had to get to the truth."

"So that's what you were going for? Truth?"

Incredulous, he stared back at her. "Of course it was. Just what are you saying?"

Allison shook her head, regret—or maybe it was pity—plain on her face. "Whose truth were you going for?"

"The suspect's."

"She'd already told you her story. She'd come back to face the consequences of her actions. Wasn't that enough?"

Because his hands were tempted to fist at his sides, Brock buried them in his uniform pockets. "I told you I was doing my job."

She only tilted her head to the side and studied him. "Did you really think by attacking that troubled girl you could change history and bring your mother back?"

"That's ridiculous—"

"Is it? You accuse Madeline of being heartless, but maybe you should look at yourself. You've worked so hard to lock everyone who loves you out that you can't even see hurt in others. That girl was hurting, and all you wanted to do was lock her up along with the ghosts of your past. Will you ever stop being that abandoned little boy?"

As Allison's car pulled away, Brock was certain a part of his heart had gone with her, ripped clean from his chest. Her disappointment in him, plus his own, stayed firmly with him even after her taillights were no longer visible.

He stood on the empty sidewalk watching after her, as if he expected her to turn around and come back to tell him everything was okay. She wouldn't be back. Sure, he would see her again. In this small town, she wouldn't be able to avoid him completely, even if she tried.

And she would try. She wouldn't laugh with him or touch him or challenge him to be a better man—someone she deserved. She wouldn't look at him that longing way she sometimes did when she didn't know he was watching—as if she just might love him. Never again would she kiss him and make him wish he believed in happy endings.

Until this moment, he hadn't even realized how much he wanted all those things, or how much he wanted Allison. Now the thought of his life without her seemed unbearable.

With his spiteful actions, he'd just proven he wasn't worthy of her. He should have known that all along. Where he was selfish, she was giving. Her faith in God was limitless, but his couldn't have been more finite. While she expected people to do the right thing, he spent all of his time waiting for the other shoe to drop.

Which one of us was right? The side of his mouth lifted to spite him. Tracie Long had come back just as Allison had expected her to, and Brock had only wanted to see her rot in jail.

So much of what Allison had said about him was true. All of it. Naked, raw truth, the type he was accustomed to tossing into suspects' faces but wasn't used to seeing it come flying back at him. And it hurt.

No one enjoyed discovering he was transparent, and yet Allison had seen right through him. The worst part was there was so much to see. She was right. He had tried to punish Madeline for her sins by showing Tracie no mercy.

Strange how he hated people who played the victim when he'd filled that role for so long that he couldn't separate himself from it. How tightly he'd held on to his pain. He'd been afraid of giving love without reservation for fear that those he loved would run out on him.

Because of his fears, he'd pushed people away. He'd pushed Allison away when his instinct told him to gather her near to his heart and to cherish her there forever. In pushing, his heart had become hard. Now his self-preservation plan had caused him to lose the one person he truly loved.

He didn't deserve her, but that didn't make him need her any less. *A day late and a dollar short.* How ironic that he was finally ready to trust when no one was asking him to. To offer his whole heart to someone when no one was waiting to accept it.

Too late. The words became chain mail, weighing on his shoulders. The blame, the hurt and guilt—they were all too heavy. Whether or not he could ever convince Allison to give him another chance, he couldn't go on carrying this deadweight.

Lord, we haven't talked in a while, so this might be too much to ask, but I need Your help, he began, the prayer feeling rusty. Still, he was certain he'd been heard. He'd always known where to take his burden, so, he wondered now, why it had taken him so long.

He couldn't allow himself to worry about how little faith he'd had, not when Jesus had said that someone with faith as small as a mustard seed could move mountains. His parents had taught him that—his *real* parents, the ones who had loved and raised him.

He'd probably destroyed every chance for being with Allison, and the pain of it felt unbearable, but he would go forward with God's help. For the first time, he laid the whole situation in God's hands.

Allison raced into her office the next morning, hoping to collect her case file and make it to the courthouse on time, despite the queasy stomach that had her running late. Facing Brock this morning in the courtroom would probably be one of the hardest things she'd ever have to do.

To be so close to him and yet know he could never be hers seemed like a happy ending as viewed through frosted glass. Would she ever stop feeling cheated by her decision to keep them apart?

Grabbing the file, she hurried toward the door, preparing herself for a negative outcome at court. Funny how she'd come to expect the worst rather than the best these past few days. She wasn't sure anymore whether good really did prevail or whether love conquered all.

She'd almost made it out of the office when the phone rang. Her pulse tripped against her will and shamed her. She had no reason to assume Brock would call her here, especially now. If he did, she was afraid that hearing his voice would be like rubbing salt in her fresh wounds.

On the third ring, she gave in and answered. "Division of Family and Children Services. May I help you?"

"Are you on your way to the courthouse?" Clara's voice came through the receiver. "I'll save you a trip. The prosecutor is not filing charges against Tracie Long."

"Are you serious? That's wonderful."

For once, the justice system seemed to have provided

real justice. She felt guilty that she could breathe only one sigh of relief on the troubled teen's behalf before releasing a second one for herself. She might not have been able to avoid seeing Brock in Destiny forever, but maybe she could keep her distance for a few days, while the wound was still so new.

"Wait. Why the change? When I talked to the prosecutor's office yesterday, they were pretty sure—"

"Don't know," her boss answered on a sigh. "Found some decency, maybe."

Allison smiled into the receiver. She doubted Brock's reaction to the prosecutor's decision would be as solidly in Tracie's court as Clara's reaction had been. She wondered whether he would take the girl's release as a personal affront just as he had internalized Joy's abandonment. Christina Marie, she corrected herself.

"Is Tracie going to do a voluntary termination of parental rights?"

"I haven't heard." Clara paused as she was wont to do with her family case managers before she gave them a new assignment. "But, Allison, there's one thing I have heard. Deputy Brock Chandler approached the prosecutor and spoke on Tracie Long's behalf."

Chapter Eleven

Two hours had passed since her enlightening telephone conversation with her boss, yet Allison's mind still swam with the knowledge that Brock had been the one to come to Tracie's defense.

She'd tried burying herself in her case files, planning some of her regular foster home visits, but her thoughts had continually returned to Brock and Tracie and the baby whose future would forever be affected by their decisions. If she hadn't been in love with Brock before, she would have fallen willingly during those two hours where thoughts of him filled her mind and heart. How she would act on her feelings, she wasn't sure, but she didn't bother denying them anymore.

"Allison." The administrative assistant stood in the doorway between the entry and the main office. "Your eleven-thirty has arrived. A new foster parent applicant."

"Could you send her in, please?"

The corner of the woman's mouth pulled up slightly. "Him."

Allison lifted an eyebrow but nodded. Couples were common applicants, as were single women, but single males were rare.

The assistant turned her head to the side. "Sir, you may go in now."

She heard a rustle of movement and the footsteps on the creaky floor, but no voice. Allison stared at the doorway and waited, keeping her expression professional.

But the form that filled the doorway stole her breath and her professional demeanor. His was the same face she expected to see in her dreams for the rest of her life.

"Brock, what are you doing here?" She wished she could hide the stark need that had to be imprinted on her face. "Do you want to be a foster parent?"

"That's part of it." His smile faltered, as if he wasn't quite sure of himself. "You're the other part."

"I don't understand." The problem was she did, or at least her hopeful heart was tempted to believe and to lay itself open to him.

Brock took several steps toward her and took both of her hands in his. "Will you give me a chance to explain?"

She nodded, emotion welling in her throat. The last tiny strings of her defenses snapped, leaving her vulnerable, her heart fragile.

He led her over to two chairs, indicating for her to take one, and he sat in the other. For several seconds, he stared at the ground, but when he spoke, he met her gaze.

"I held on to the blame I felt for my birth mother too

long, but I've finally let it go. I never realized how that blame held my heart captive."

She opened her mouth to tell him he was wrong, to try to soften the stark truth, but he only shook his head.

"I don't want to be judge and jury for other people's lives anymore, based on my own mother's poor decision. I have no right. I never did. I was wrong."

Allison grasped his hands. "You were hurting."

"That's no excuse. I can't give myself one when I wouldn't give anyone else one."

"How can you say that? You convinced the prosecutor not to charge Tracie."

"That was because of you. You always believed."

Allison smiled as she released his hands. "She loves her baby."

"I know. I met with her and her parents last night. She wanted to do the right thing."

Something warm expanded inside of her. He had compassion after all. It just took him a while to find it.

She must have been smiling off into the distance because he took her hands again to get her attention. "Allison, I asked Tracie for her forgiveness last night. Now I want to ask for yours. Can you forgive me?"

At her nod he sighed. "Phew, that's a relief, because I want to ask you for something else. Would you take a chance on us? There's something good growing between us, and I feel God's leading to build upon it."

Allison gasped, but the air felt good hitting the suddenly dry back of her throat. So this was what it felt like to have everything she'd ever wanted laid out within her grasp. She'd questioned it before, but she was certain now that Brock was the man God had planned for her. This had been His plan all along.

Brock could see it, the way the hope seemed to bloom in Allison's expression, in the glow of her lovely skin, in the way her posture relaxed. He understood it because he felt it, too, sensed that today would be the beginning of all things good for the both of them.

He grinned. "Should I take that smile as a maybe?"

"Take it as a yes."

He knew he should stop. It was too much too soon. Yet he couldn't. He wanted more. All. He'd spent a lifetime doing the wrong thing, so why should he waste a moment of doing the right one? He would wait on her if she wanted him to. Her needs mattered more than his. He owed his new life to her, and now he wanted to give her his.

"Allison, this is crazy. I know it's too soon to tell you this, but I'm in love with you." His pulse raced, and his palms dampened, but he felt compelled to go on. "I think Tracie is right. God does have a plan for Joy. I think he wants us to build a family for her. Just the three of us."

Her eyes widened, but they glistened, making him wonder if she would tearfully reject him. It probably was a little late for him to suggest that they go out on a first date or something. You know, take it slow.

What would he do if she turned him down when everything inside him told him God's purpose for his life was to love her? Could he live without her?

But Allison only quirked an eyebrow. "Are you asking me to marry you?"

"I can't imagine living my life without you. I could wait another six months and ask again if that's what you want, but I want to be your husband now, six months from now and sixty years from now."

She studied him for several seconds. "But you are asking...right this minute?"

"Let's just say, for reference sake, if I *were* asking today, what would your answer be?"

She tapped her index finger to her chin and squeezed her eyes shut, appearing to ponder, before she opened them again. "Okay, then, for reference sake, I'd say yes."

"Then that makes this a whole lot easier." He lowered on one knee right there in front of the office assistant, the other caseworker and their boss who were crowded in the doorway now. "Allison, I love you. Please be my wife and help me become a better man."

Her eyes shone with tears again, but she smiled as they spilled over. "Yes, I'll marry you but only because I love you. I don't want to fix you. I want to make a life with you."

"It's a deal then." Brock reached out his hand as if to shake hers, but when she offered hers, he lifted it to his lips and gently kissed it. Then he stood and drew her into his arms where she belonged. As his lips touched hers again, the promise of his heart so plainly offered with them, he had the sensation of a homecoming from a long, hard journey.

When he pulled his head away, her eyes appeared glazed with the intoxication of their blooming love. Her eyes were probably a mirror of his own.

"Oh, I have one more question. Would it be okay if we get married this afternoon? I've reserved Judge Douglas's court at four-thirty."

She let out a laugh. "Were you that sure I would accept?"

"Not sure. I hoped." *Hoped.* It was the same thing Allison had said about delaying the court hearing while waiting for Joy's mother to return. Because of Allison, he had learned to hope, as well.

"Were you hoping, too, that I didn't have my heart set on a big church wedding?" She cocked her head to the side.

"We can be married at church later—as big as you want—but would you mind making it legal today? I want to put 'Married' on my foster parent application." He stopped himself and shook his head. "No, it wouldn't matter if Joy wasn't even in the picture. I would still want to marry you today because I can't wait to be your husband."

She was chuckling now. "But you were serious about becoming a foster parent? You'll be required to complete twenty hours of training, get agency approval and have a home study completed. I'll have to quit my job because of the conflict of interest."

Brock's breath caught in his throat. "What do you think? Is it all too much, too fast?"

She didn't hesitate at all before she shook her head. "You're right. I believe Joy belongs with us. I think God planned it from the beginning. But more than that, I think God wants me to be with you, today and always."

* * *

Allison stood outside the courtroom door, Clara fixing the tiny veil on her pillbox hat. Fortunately, for her, she and her boss were the same size, and Clara had possessed elegantly simple taste when she'd married.

"You look wonderful," Clara marveled. "It's mostly the suit."

Allison grinned. "Thanks for the vote of confidence."

If she looked half as good on the outside as she felt on the inside, then she had to be glowing. Her hands brushed down the short jacket of her winter white bridal suit, amazed at how much had been accomplished in the past five hours. She could barely catch her breath.

She wasn't sure she even wanted to. By the end of this single day she would have become a fiancée, a wife, a *former* family case manager and a potential regular foster parent.

Had there been a waiting period for a marriage license, they would never have made it. All she had to do was show proof of immunization for rubella, and they were signing the document.

It only seemed an appropriate step in their whirlwind romance to marry so quickly. Well, fast or incredibly slow, she was convinced they would end up in the same place: together.

At the sound of pounding footsteps, Allison turned to see David rushing down the hall. "You made it."

Her best friend swiped his forehead with the handkerchief from his suit. "Barely. Ever heard of planning ahead?"

"That's for amateurs."

"Are you sure this is what you want? Isn't it a little… sudden? I was trying to encourage you to get started dating, but you leapt right past dinner and a movie to flowers and a cake."

Allison laughed and hugged her dear friend. "If I believed my feelings for Brock would change one bit if I waited a month or a year, I'd do it. But this is God's plan. I've never been more certain of anything."

David hugged her again. "Maybe someday I'll find someone who makes me glow the way Brock does you."

"You will. In His time."

The door opened, and one of Brock's friends from the sheriff's department popped his head out. "You guys ready?"

"On our way," David announced, holding out his arm so he could escort her into the courtroom.

Surprisingly, the room wasn't empty as she'd expected, but full of standing friends—the cast from the live nativity, fellow church members, a few sheriff's deputies and some foster parents with their foster kids. Most shocking of all, instead of being back in Ohio, Tracie and her parents sat in the front row.

Only when everyone else sat could she see Brock, looking amazing in a great-fitting suit. The other people around them blurred as she saw only him.

"No cold feet?" he asked when she'd reached him and David had handed her into her groom's care.

"Didn't have time for it."

"That was my plan all along."

Judge Douglas's legal service was short and direct, but Allison didn't really hear it, anyway. She saw Brock and no one else. As they traded gold bands—a purchase from early that afternoon—she couldn't hold back her tears. Dreams she'd thought impossible fell into place with a gentle, chaste kiss.

Too soon it was over, and friends were crowding around them, offering their best wishes. Last of all, she found herself in Tracie's tearful embrace.

"I knew God had a plan for Christina," Tracie whispered. "I realize now it's with the both of you. I've already told the judge that I'd like you two to adopt, but I don't know what will happen when I sign the papers."

"Everything will be fine," Allison answered, convinced of it. Still, tears streamed down her face. "I'll try to love her as much as you do."

Brock came up from behind and put his arm around Allison. "Tracie, are you making my bride cry?"

The teen smiled through her own tears. "Only from happiness."

"That's the only reason she'll ever have to cry again." He bent his head and dropped a loving kiss on his new wife's temple. Both hugged the teen once more, and Tracie's parents led her out of the courtroom.

Allison watched after her. "It was so hard for Tracie to do what she believes is the right thing."

Brock lifted his thumb and wiped a tear that trailed down her cheek. "Yes, it was. But I know that even Tracie wouldn't want you to be crying on your wedding day. Now I have a surprise for you, Mrs. Chandler."

He indicated with his head toward the far corner of the room where foster mother Margaret Ross had entered and was swaying and cooing to the baby. Margaret hurried over and lowered the sleeping infant into Allison's arms.

As if the guests recognized the three of them needed a few moments alone since it would be a while before they could legally be together, they exited to the courthouse hall.

Once they were alone, Brock leaned forward and kissed the baby's brow. "Did you tell Tracie we're planning to change her name when the adoption is final?"

She shook her head. "I didn't think the time was right. She was having a hard enough time saying goodbye."

"I'm sure she'll be pleased with the name. Christina Joy is perfect." He brushed his thumb along the baby's jawline. "It doesn't matter anyway. Everyone will always call her Joy."

"It's who she is."

Brock leaned in close to press his lips to Allison's, the kiss seeming to join the three of them together in a promise. They were not yet a family, but with God's help, one day they would be. Longing brought the newlyweds still closer until Joy squirmed and grunted. They laughed together and, with Brock's arm around the two females in his life, they left the courtroom.

As soon as they reached the hall, the crowd broke out into a post-Christmas rendition of "Joy to the World." Allison only smiled, feeling Brock's grip tighten on her shoulder. It couldn't have been a better wedding recessional. Joy. Her heart swelled with the emotion she'd never thought would be hers.

With reluctance, Allison handed the child back to Margaret, hoping it would only be temporary.

Brock took the opportunity to turn Allison into his embrace. For several minutes, they simply stood and held each other. By the time they let go of each other, their guests had quietly exited the courthouse door.

"Do you think it will all be downhill from here?" Allison asked.

"Are you kidding? How many couples can say they've had a start like ours?"

A chuckle of happiness rose low in her throat. "Not many, I would guess."

"None."

With that he led her out of the building and into their new life together. There were still things to work out, such as how they could make Allison's mother's house into a home for them and for Joy. Allison knew that creating a home would take time and patience. The most important part was already in place. They'd already created their family together—a family formed by a child in a manger.

* * * * *

REQUEST YOUR FREE BOOKS!

2 FREE INSPIRATIONAL NOVELS
PLUS 2
FREE
MYSTERY GIFTS

Love Inspired

Name _____ (PLEASE PRINT)

Address _____ Apt. #

City _____ State/Prov. _____ Zip/Postal Code

Signature (if under 18, a parent or guardian must sign)

Mail to the Harlequin® Reader Service:
IN U.S.A.: P.O. Box 1867, Buffalo, NY 14240-1867
IN CANADA: P.O. Box 609, Fort Erie, Ontario L2A 5X3

**Are you a subscriber to Love Inspired books
and want to receive the larger-print edition?
Call 1-800-873-8635 or visit www.ReaderService.com.**

REQUEST YOUR FREE BOOKS!

2 FREE INSPIRATIONAL NOVELS
PLUS 2
FREE
MYSTERY GIFTS

Love Inspired

HISTORICAL

INSPIRATIONAL HISTORICAL ROMANCE

YES! Please send me 2 FREE Love Inspired® Historical novels and my 2 FREE mystery gifts (gifts are worth about $10). After receiving them, if I don't wish to receive any more books, I can return the shipping statement marked "cancel." If I don't cancel, I will receive 4 brand-new novels every month and be billed just $4.49 per book in the U.S. or $4.99 per book in Canada. That's a savings of at least 22% off the cover price. It's quite a bargain! Shipping and handling is just 50¢ per book in the U.S. and 75¢ per book in Canada.* I understand that accepting the 2 free books and gifts places me under no obligation to buy anything. I can always return a shipment and cancel at any time. Even if I never buy another book, the two free books and gifts are mine to keep forever.

102/302 IDN FV2V

Name _____
(PLEASE PRINT)

Address _____ Apt. #

City _____ State/Prov. _____ Zip/Postal Code

Signature (if under 18, a parent or guardian must sign)

Mail to the Harlequin® Reader Service:
IN U.S.A.: P.O. Box 1867, Buffalo, NY 14240-1867
IN CANADA: P.O. Box 609, Fort Erie, Ontario L2A 5X3

Want to try two free books from another series?
Call 1-800-873-8635 or visit www.ReaderService.com.

* Terms and prices subject to change without notice. Prices do not include applicable taxes. Sales tax applicable in N.Y. Canadian residents will be charged applicable taxes. Offer not valid in Quebec. This offer is limited to one order per household. Not valid for current subscribers to Love Inspired Historical books. All orders subject to credit approval. Credit or debit balances in a customer's account(s) may be offset by any other outstanding balance owed by or to the customer. Please allow 4 to 6 weeks for delivery. Offer available while quantities last.

Your Privacy—The Harlequin® Reader Service is committed to protecting your privacy. Our Privacy Policy is available online at www.ReaderService.com or upon request from the Harlequin Reader Service.

We make a portion of our mailing list available to reputable third parties that offer products we believe may interest you. If you prefer that we not exchange your name with third parties, or if you wish to clarify or modify your communication preferences, please visit us at www.ReaderService.com/consumerschoice or write to us at Harlequin Reader Service Preference Service, P.O. Box 9062, Buffalo, NY 14269. Include your complete name and address.

LIHDIR13

REQUEST YOUR FREE BOOKS!

2 FREE RIVETING INSPIRATIONAL NOVELS
PLUS 2 FREE MYSTERY GIFTS

Love Inspired®
SUSPENSE

LISDIR13